The Petrified World

and other tales

A collection of short stories in support of Population Matters

Edited by Martin Pond

ISBN: 9781731553966

Edited by Martin Pond.

With thanks to the authors, all of whom have given their time and effort freely.

CONTENTS

INTRODUCTION

Martin Pond

It's a good time to be a reader, and a writer, of short stories. Or, as Neil Gaiman once memorably called them "the novel's wayward younger brother". From a position, not so long ago, when the main outlets for short stories were closing or scaling back, the digital revolution has completely changed the publishing landscape. Rather than finish off those traditional outlets, new technology has enabled readers to consume short stories in new ways, and enabled anyone to be a publisher. There are now, perhaps, more outlets for short stories than there have ever been.

In short, the population of those wayward younger brothers is booming.

Of course, it is not alone. Our global population is also booming, in a way that makes the growth in short stories seem pedestrian. As I write this, there are more than 7.5 billion people on planet Earth, a number currently growing at a rate of a billion every twelve to fifteen years. The United Nations conservatively estimates a population of nearly 9.8bn by 2050 – 30% higher than it is today. And according to the Global Footprint Network, we already use the renewable resources of 1.7 Earths, so how are we going to manage in 2050, and beyond?

The Food and Agriculture Organization estimates that we will need 70% more food by 2050, whilst waterfootprint.org estimates that, by then, four billion people will live in areas that are short of water. I could go on, easily, with other equally shocking models and predictions, none of which are wild guesses but peer-reviewed and science-based. But I don't need to go on, not when esteemed naturalist and broadcaster Sir David Attenborough has already encapsulated the issue so well when he said:

"All environmental problems become harder – and ultimately impossible – to solve with ever more people."

The Earth's present rate of population growth is unsustainable; in light of this, the charity Population Matters believes that, for the Earth to provide for us all, we must reduce our impact as a species, and that those of us who are wealthy must reduce it drastically as soon as we can. There are many ways in which we can and must do that but the single most effective and immediate way of reducing our consumption and our impact is to reduce the number of consumers by having smaller families. Each person born has an impact over their entire lifespan and if they have children themselves, that impact is magnified. Fewer people being born eases the pressure on our planet, reducing our emissions and pollution, conserving our resources and bringing us back into balance with the natural world.

Of course, this is a provocative standpoint - many people do not want to face up to a seemingly insurmountable problem, whilst the merest mention of population being an issue summons up past, failed approaches such as China's one-child policy. Managing our global population responsibly has become a controversial topic, over-simplistically and wrongly equated with the ideas of coercion or constraining the rights of parents and families. And so the spiralling growth in our numbers has become the elephant in the room - it's obvious it's there but no-one wants to deal with it. To question the wisdom of large families has become almost a taboo. This issue, which should regularly be on our front pages, has become a hidden subject. The words that need to be said have become unspoken.

This collection takes the idea of taboos, of hidden subjects, of unspoken truths, as its loose theme. Some of the stories address potential problems for a near-future Earth, some do not, but all are linked by the idea of what is *not* being talked about, whether that's between families, colleagues, in the news or on a wider scale.

All of these stories have been given freely in support of this collection, profits from which will be donated to Population Matters - once you have read them, why not take a moment to read more about the underlying issues, and what you can do to help, at www.populationmatters.org

The Petrified World and other tales

THE PETRIFIED WORLD

Mark Kilner

It had been, she thought to herself as she snapped another leg off the wooden coffee table, a very quiet apocalypse. The sky hadn't fallen in, the mountains hadn't crumbled, the oceans hadn't boiled, and there was a welcome absence of marauding giant robots and flesh-eating zombies. The fall of civilisation had happened quickly and with a minimum of fuss. You could almost say it was a *civilised* way to end.

She tossed the table-leg onto the hearth (in the absence of electricity or gas she'd had to break into nearly a dozen houses before she found one with a traditional open fireplace) and looked at the stone figures on the other side of the living room. They were huddled together on the sofa, a middle-aged couple staring sightlessly at their television. In the cold grey light of day they'd looked like sculptures that had been misplaced from an art gallery, but now, in the flickering firelight, they seemed almost on the verge of returning to life.

"I don't know what they called you," she said to the dog

curled up at her feet, "but I think I might name you Bowie." The dog, a black and white collie with strikingly mismatched eyes, pricked up its ears and then dropped them again. It had been understandably wary of her at first, but some soothing words and the smell of food had quickly turned it into an ally. She wondered about all the other dogs trapped in homes that had abruptly become prisons, and then she thought of all the starving infants lying helplessly in their cots, their desperate cries going unheeded as their calcified parents gazed with unseeing eyes into black mirrors. Then she started to think of all the homes with babies *and* dogs, but the implications of that scenario were too horrible to contemplate. Perhaps her "quiet" apocalypse was less civilised than she cared to admit.

The fire crackled and spat embers into the flue, providing a merciful distraction. "I'm sorry for invading your house and eating your food," she murmured to the stone couple, "but I promise I'll look after your dog. Does that sound reasonable?" The stone woman's wedding ring glinted in the firelight and her hand strayed to her own symbol of attachment: a diamond engagement ring, a reminder of a promise made on a beach guarded by statues of a more conventional origin. She pushed the memory away before it had a chance to drown out her other thoughts. There would be a time and a place to address such matters. But not here. Not now.

She left the house before dawn; a satchel slung over one shoulder and a rucksack on her back, weighed down with bottled water and tinned rations. The dog trotted at her side, happy to be outdoors. A stone postman waited for them outside the gate. He was clutching his phone in his hand, a trolley full of undelivered mail standing behind him. The dog paused to urinate against his leg – the canine equivalent of a last laugh, she supposed – and then they walked along the old footpath until she had a clear view across the fields towards the mudflats and the sea beyond. The usual soundtrack of modern life had gone. There were no voices, no traffic, no planes flying overhead; just the gentle whisper of the wind brushing over the tops of the cauliflowers and a few hesitant snatches of birdsong signalling the slow creep towards spring.

A few days ago she had been living an unremarkable life as a programmer in a bustling, noisy world that was utterly indifferent to her. Now that world had been silenced, its inhabitants transformed into statues staring blankly at their prized gadgets, a civilisation locked in time by an apocalypse no one had seen coming. They were victims of the first virus to jump from computers to humans, the first virus to cross the seemingly unbridgeable divide between digital and biological. But that was as much as anyone knew, or would ever know. Such things weren't supposed to happen in this supposedly enlightened age, but the proof of it was written in stone. No wonder the emergency radio broadcasts had informally named it the Medusa Virus.

She remembered how the usually unflappable BBC announcers had struggled to hide the fear in their voices. On day one they issued an emergency broadcast advising the public not to look at their phones, their computers, or their TVs, but the warning was already too late. The virus was propagating into every corner of cyberspace and even the experts had underestimated the extent to which the internet had hooked its claws into everyday life. On day two the broadcasts warned the public to keep away from built-up areas and major roads. On day three they warned the public to stay indoors and stay calm.

Then the radios fell silent.

She lingered, hoping to see the sun rise over this new world, but a sea mist was rolling in ahead of it, merging smoothly into the pale tangerine sky.

She turned her back on the sunrise, and on her old,

unremarkable life.

She and the dog cut across a golf course, using the morning mist as cover. No doubt there were other survivors in this strange new world, people who had somehow managed to avoid exposure to the virus, but she had no desire to join forces with them. They'd want to rebuild, to put things back *the way they were*. The thought of it appalled her.

Two figures loomed out of the murk, a pair of unwary golfers who had been caught checking their phones between shots. Now they were frozen in time just like everyone else, sculptured men on a sculptured green. It reminded her of that beach again: a windswept expanse with a hundred cast-iron figures embedded in the sand, all of them facing the sea as the tide ebbed and flowed around them. Only a year had passed since that day, but now it seemed like a whole other lifetime ago.

She looked into the eyes of one of the stone golfers, trying to read his expression, but his face was a benign death-mask, betraying no clue as to what he had seen on his phone. Whatever he'd been in life was no longer relevant. Now he was like those figures on the beach: just another exhibit in a world-wide art installation.

Am I a survivor or a curator? she wondered.

They left the golfers behind, and eventually the sun began to break through the murk, casting her shadow in front of her. She stopped to take a battery pack out of her jacket pocket, opening the case to reveal a small trifold solar array. Then she clipped it to the outside of her backpack, angling it towards the sun. It wasn't very efficient, but it was good enough. She only had one device she needed to keep charged, one she didn't intend to use unless there was no other choice.

They walked on. The farther she travelled the more she felt as if she was a part of the landscape instead of just a passive observer. She imagined herself becoming absorbed into every leaf and every blade of grass, her ego dissipating into the wind like the morning mist. If this was to be her passage into oblivion then she welcomed it. She'd rather be remembered in birdsong and spring flowers than condemned to the inert obscurity of carved stone.

She decided it would be quicker and simpler to follow the railway line the rest of the way to the city, but they'd have to cross the dual carriageway to reach it. She crept up to the edge of the embankment, using her binoculars to scan for movement among the stranded cars. A few buzzards and crows circled above the road, but otherwise it was still and silent. On the horizon she could see the endpoint of her metaphorical pilgrimage: the distinctive outline of the cathedral protruding from the city skyline into the hazy sky. She lowered the binoculars and waited, allowing time for her senses to tune into the new surroundings.

After a few minutes she nodded to the dog and together they scrambled down the embankment. Here was confirmation, as if it were needed, of why she couldn't just drive across the county. A few of the cars had managed to pull over to the hard shoulder, but many of them had simply crumpled into each other, effectively turning both sides of the carriageway into one long, impassable breaker's yard.

As she clambered over the central reservation she saw a stone driver sitting behind the wheel of his HGV, his sightless eyes forever locked on his sat-nav display. He was one of the lucky ones. Not all the victims had been petrified before they crashed, and she quickly averted her eyes from the bodies trapped in their mangled cars. Others had managed to crawl or stagger free, only to be transformed the moment they tried to call for help, the fear and confusion preserved on their faces like the ancient victims of Pompeii. She craned her neck to look up, but that only made her think of all the planes that were now absent from the sky. She imagined them plunging towards the sea as they ran out of fuel, oxygen masks dangling uselessly in front of the passengers' stone, placid faces.

"Help me." The voice was so quiet she wondered if she had imagined it, but the dog's ears were up, listening. Then she heard it again: "Please help me." There was a man watching her from the broken window of one of the crashed cars. He had been pinned to his seat by the steering wheel and she wondered how he'd managed to survive so long, but as she drew closer she saw the plastic bottle of water in his free hand. His other arm was bent at an unpleasant angle, the fingers hooked into claws.

"I thought I was the only one," the man gasped. His face was as grey as the suit he was wearing; a commuter suspended en route to a job that no longer existed. "I don't know what happened. We were driving and then everyone just started to …" His voice faltered and he blinked away tears. "I thought I was dead."

You might as well be, she thought. She tried to open the door but the force of the impact had jammed it into the centre pillar. It would need specialist tools to break it free, the kind that were no longer in use.

"My phone was on the passenger seat," the man said. "It's gone. I don't know where it went." Almost as an afterthought he added, "I can't feel my legs."

"I can't get you out of there," she replied. "And even if I could, I wouldn't be able to carry you."

The man grimaced. "Please. I have money. Let me use your phone."

"Money's no good anymore. And there's no one left to call." She took the satchel off her shoulder and opened it carefully, holding the contents up in front of the man's face.

"What are you doing?"

"You asked me to help you, and that's what I'm going to

do. In the only way I can."

The weather had deteriorated by the time they reached the city centre; rain glistened on the faces of the statues, imbuing them with a dark lustre. The high street held the largest concentration of statues she had seen so far: stone figures of all ages surrounded them; some gazing into cashpoints or shop window displays, most of them gazing at their phones. She felt like the last survivor of a civilisation that had been simultaneously fossilised and memorialised, a civilisation that had been granted a kind of immortality – but one that came at a cruel price. She walked past a small group of stone tourists all striking poses for a phone held on an outstretched stick. Maybe this is how it was always going to end, she thought to herself. Not with a bang or a whimper, but with a selfie.

She approached a department store. Clothed statues and clothed mannequins stood on either side of the glass, each wearing the same blank stares of indifference. Eventually nature would reclaim these urbanised spaces. The statues would become artefacts, strangled by weeds and blotted by lichen like old gravestones, eroded and smoothed by years of rain and wind and baking heat and biting cold until the death masks became rough approximations of faces. In time a lot of the statues would topple over. The phones would fall from their unfeeling fingers and their clothes would rot away, leaving behind stone nudes gazing at their empty hands as if they were trying to read a lost future from the faint lines engraved into their worn stone palms. She wondered how future historians would interpret these mysterious figures. What would they read into their chipped faces, their outstretched hands, their ambiguous postures?

The dog let out a low growl, breaking her reverie. She looked along the street and noticed that some of the statues had already been stripped of their clothes. Others had been defaced: their mouths smeared with lipstick; crude epithets daubed onto their foreheads. A little farther on she found a statue that was missing both of its arms, a contemporary *Venus de Milo.* She advanced carefully, keeping to the shadows at the side of the street. Clearly there were other survivors at large in the city, ones whom she had no intention of interacting with. She wondered what had prompted such needless acts of vandalism. Perhaps, like her, they harboured an irrational fear that the statues might suddenly spring back to life.

Twenty minutes later she and the dog were standing inside a smartly furnished terraced house – *his* house. As she'd anticipated, it was impossibly tidy, more like a display home than a place where people actually lived.

But at least it had a fireplace.

She placed her foot on the bottom stair and then hesitated, her hand resting on the banister. The dog looked at her, ears cocked as if to say, *What are you going to do?*

I'm going to see it through to the end, she told herself. *I didn't come all this way just to chicken out.*

"Wait here," she said to the dog, and then she crept upstairs and pushed open the bedroom door. The woman – she couldn't bring herself to use her name – was lying in bed, her stone fingers curled around her phone, her once lustrous blonde hair draped across the pillow like opaque strands of glass fibre. But there was no one with her.

Her breath caught in her throat and for a moment she too became a statue. He wasn't here; she'd have to start over, painstakingly searching the local pubs, his office, his friends' homes, all the other places he might be. But then she noticed a pair of men's socks on the bedroom floor. She crossed to the bathroom, forced the door open and there he was: the man who'd turned her heart to stone. He was sitting on the toilet, his trousers around his stone ankles, his expressionless eyes fixed intently on the phone clutched in his cold grey fingers. He too had been memorialised, but in a most undignified manner.

She'd been holding the memories at bay, but now they came flooding back. She remembered all of it: the long train journey to Liverpool, the scent of the rose petals scattered on the hotel bed, the walk along Crosby Beach with all those iron figures silhouetted against the pink light of the setting sun, how he'd steered her towards that one particular statue with the ring already concealed in the palm of its hand. "I'm not leaving this beach till you say yes," he'd told her, his knee slowly sinking into the wet sand. "Even if it means I have to stay here with these statues forever."

She carefully eased the phone out of his stone hand and placed it face-down on the floor. Then she removed her diamond ring and pushed it onto his little finger, twisting it as far as it would go. "You can have this back," she said into the stone hollow of his ear. "Give it to your new flame – if you ever make it off the toilet."

She returned downstairs and prepared some food while the dog watched her, its head resting on its paws. She spooned jelly-encased chunks of rabbit into a bowl and its ears drooped.

"That's as good as it gets until we hit another store," she said. "If you don't like it, catch a fresh one and I'll cook that for you." The words were accompanied by a half-smile, but there would come a time when it would no longer be a joke. It wasn't always going to be this comfortable; of that she was under no illusions. She studied the best-before date on the lid of the tin. Two years. That was probably her upper limit. Two years to learn how to become self-sufficient. Two years for the scavenger to become a hunter-gatherer.

She got the fire going and used it to toast some marshmallows, smearing them with jam. The dog abandoned its dinner and watched her, a thin line of drool trailing from the side of its mouth. "Don't look at me like that," she said, but she knew she was going to end up giving the dog one of the marshmallows. The dog knew it too.

She followed the marshmallows with apricots, spooning them straight from the tin. When the tin was half full she poured in some condensed milk, stirring it into the juice before eating the rest of the fruit. Finally she boiled some water in a saucepan and made coffee, cupping her hands around the mug to warm her fingers.

Afterwards she collapsed on the sofa and closed her eyes, listening to the rain pattering against the window. The dog clambered up beside her, bringing a smile to her lips. Rose petals were one thing, but *he* would have hated to see dog-hairs on the furniture.

It was night when they left the house. The city was shrouded in the darkness of a permanent blackout. The rain clouds had cleared too; she could see the familiar patterns of Cassiopeia and Perseus high overhead, shining brightly in the unpolluted sky.

The dog growled suddenly and she glimpsed figures moving in the shadows on the opposite side of the street. Damn. She'd lingered in one place for too long and now there were going to be consequences. The confrontation she'd been at pains to avoid had become a reality.

One of the figures flicked on a torch. There were four of them: three men and one woman. "Don't be afraid," the first man said. "You should come with us. It's not safe out here."

Safe for whom? she wondered, but she said nothing. She shone her own torch across the figures, looking for signs of duress in the woman's face, but she saw only her own wariness reflected back at her.

"There's so few of us left," one of the other men said. "We need to stick together."

Keeping the torch moving across their faces, she casually reached down with her other hand and loosened the straps on her satchel until the flap fell down, exposing the dark screen of the tablet. Her thumb settled in the smooth hollow of the Home button. She'd practiced this manoeuvre so many times she could do it with her eyes closed (which was, perhaps, the only *truly* safe way to do it), but she'd never had to do it like this, with so much at stake. It had worked on the poor man in the car, but would it work from this range? She quickly considered her other options. She was willing to fight if necessary, but there was no way she could take on all four of them, even with the dog to back her up. She doubted she could outrun them either, and the noise might attract others.

The woman laughed nervously. "Are we just going to stand here all night?"

"So go back to where you came from," she replied. "I'm not stopping you."

"Hey, we're all on the same side here." One of the men moved his hand towards his pocket and that was enough to settle it for her. She spun on her heels, bringing the tablet round to face them, and she saw the light from the screen play across their faces as she pushed the button. She blinked and in that moment – the fraction of a second it took for her eyelids to close and open again – four people of flesh and blood became four people of stone. The dog approached the nearest one, sniffed its leg cautiously, and then cocked its head to one side, puzzled by this turn of events.

Why couldn't you leave me alone? she thought as she switched the tablet off and returned it to the safety of her satchel. *Why couldn't you all just leave me in peace?* She wondered what the man had been reaching for in his pocket and she was in the process of reaching for it herself when she decided against it. There was nothing to gain from that knowledge but vindication or guilt, and she could live without either of those things. Choosing *not* to look was what had kept her alive this long; it might just keep her sane too.

She let her hand fall to her side and looked to the sky again. She realised now just how much of her life she had spent relying on others to make the decisions, reacting instead of acting, answering questions instead of posing them. A lifetime of being ignored and overlooked and let down by broken promises.

"Do you see me now?" she whispered at the stars. "Do you see the snakes in my hair, the flint in my eyes?"

Her words evaporated in the cold air and with them, her bitterness. She ruffled the dog's head and together they set off along the street, leaving behind the house with its unhappy memories and the four new statues staring at a space where a woman had once stood. She'd been waiting for something to change, and now *everything* had changed. All the points on the compass were hers. Every day was hers to do with as she pleased.

And she was determined to relish every moment of it.

PIG HUNTING
An excerpt from *Out Of Nowhere*

Ian Nettleton

His old man had always had ambition. He was never bored with life. There was always some new venture, some new area of interest. Some new deal to be made. Some new horse to back. Something new to trade. Come on son, he said to Frank on that one particular night. It's time you saw what your old man does to make a living, eh.

He should have said no, he didn't want to go. He should have been asleep himself. But no, it was his old dad inviting him out into his private world. If he was to return to that night, would he have been able to say no, knowing what was to come?

The quiet Minindee streets. The old engine rumbling. His dad driving out of the town and never speaking until they were in the bush, travelling into the farming belt. Alright, son? This is it.

Yanking the wheel, turning into the side of the road and pulling up sharp.

Get out and stand by the side and don't go running off

where I can't find you.

For that was his father then, in the day of his majority, when he was strong as an iron bark and had a barrel chest and other men gravitated towards him wherever he was though he barely noticed this deference. And that day, of all days, was the last of those days. Frank remembered it most of all, above all others, the day of his father's decline.

Climbing into the roadside grass. Grasshoppers leaping away. The heat rising from the land, the fields level with the road. The clang of the door and his father walking around the front end of the ute. His breath wheezing. A sack rolled under one arm, a rifle in his hand. Standing there breathing like a pair of bellows. Nodding towards the far side of the fallow field.

We're going to catch some game. I want you to drive it towards me.

A distant hillside. Tan coloured earth and sandwich panel huts, grey troughs on wheels and, routing in the dirt, pink fleshed pigs.

Game, said Frank.

That's right.

Game's what he said. Game, like a rabbit caught in a wire at the mouth of a burrow. Like a guinea fowl shot fluttering out of the sky and wrapped in newspaper. A wild boar. See these little beauties. They're out here to farrow, yeah? Each one of these huts has a mother inside. Easy game, son.

All of it was game to you, said Frank, continuing along the embankment, passing the vehicle, yellow grass growing around its wheel arches and riding boards. Somebody drove that vehicle till it could be driven no more and abandoned it here.

At midday he found the cool shade of some brush cherries, down by a bend in a slow moving river. The water was clear to its stony bed and he scooped a handful at a time and drank and could never quite slake his thirst.

Flies in the lengths of sunlight that cut through the shadows, that stayed where they were and never bothered him. His stomach was eating itself and he took another cupped handful of water and another to fill himself.

He remembered how the young pig ran ahead, nimble and whinnying through the cropped straw and into the saplings that bordered the wood, where he could see his father crouched, the gun across his knees like a club. The pig so intent on escaping Frank, it didn't see the man and as it passed him he levelled the length of the gun and touched it to the skull, behind the pig's ear.

The sound of the gun was like the sudden puncturing of a tyre. The barrel leapt up, a flash that quickly vanished. The pig ran on but it ran sideways, crashing through the dry brush, though there was a fine red mist that fell on the floor of the wood and on the outspread leaves and pale ringed bark.

Well fuckery, said his dad, standing, his face speckled red as he turned to look at Frank. Come on then, don't let's lose him.

Running through the fine white eucalypts that stood with their serried peelings of bark, running over the sunken stones, across an open space, back into the shadows and the deeper woods, hearing the heft of the pig, seeing its shanks as it ran then tottered, then ran on again, its last burst of life. Blood running from his neck, a spattered trail along the ground. For a time he lost sight of the pig. He heard it crashing through undergrowth and behind him he heard the bellows of his father's breathing, the thump of his boots.

When he came into the open land, there across the low swale was a drinking pool, round, sloped at the edges. Tottering towards this, finally slowing, was the pig, slathered with blood and grass and hay and twigs adhered to its sweating hide. His father appeared beside him, his breathing hoarse.

Get to it. Come on.

Frank put on some speed to catch up with the pig, his father behind him, but as the pig reached the water hole it ran down the bank, its pink behind vanishing over the rim as if all it had needed was a drink.

When he reached the water, there it floated, the blood blooming like a vivid oil spill. He stood and looked as the pink corpse turned, just above the waterline, its fat belly with the swollen teats. His father arrived beside him and huffed and puffed and wheezed. He looked at Frank and he looked about him, at the open field.

There's a farmhouse.

Over by a glade of trees and a line of fence posts that ran from the main road stood a low bungalow, outhouses, a water pump and tank on stilts, an open barn and large, flat roofed pig shed.

We better get this out of here before anyone sees us. He looked about him. I left the rope in the car. He looked at Frank. Well go and get it.

The water was still and the pig turned slowly as an unanchored boat. There were dark weeds beneath the surface and the depths were black. Frank began trotting towards the woods.

Not that way. The short way.

He pointed up the incline to the road. Frank turned and began running towards the line of fences. By the time he reached the car he was bent over, his hands on his knees, tying to draw in more breath than his lungs would allow. Sweat dropped from his face into the dust at the roadside and his throat felt raw and tasted of blood.

When he had caught his breath and his lungs no longer felt as though they were stuck to his ribs he pulled open the door. The rope was coiled in the footwell and he slung it over his shoulder. It was hard and heavy.

He ran back the way he'd come, his feet slapping on the

surface of the road his own breath whistling in his throat. The heat of the day seemed to have taken most of the air, his lungs struggled and his calf muscles were beginning to ache.

When he reached the fence and the open field he stopped to rest his arms on the wire and leaned a moment, the posts swinging in the loosened earth in which they were sunk. His breath was hoarse and his heart was hammering. He saw his father who had his bush hat pressed onto his head being walked off towards the outbuildings. Walking on the one side of him was a skinny little man with a hand on the back of his neck the way an adult might guide an infant who has barely learned to walk. Separate from the two of them was another, larger man walking a little way behind. He held in his hands what looked like a rifle and two black dogs ran about them, barking at his father.

In the shade of the trees Frank looks down river where the water flows, running over the stones blackly. He turns his head another way for he cannot bear to see that diminished image of his father, walking from him. Diminished and ever after changed, for he would not see that man again.

THE TRANSISTOR

Andrea Holland

I put my fork down. Enough - no more pancake. My grandfather made breakfast as if it was the last supper. I was desperate for a smoke, but instead I sipped the coffee in the chipped Silver Jubilee mug and fiddled with my teaspoon, watching Grandad turn the radio dial in and out of fuzzy air to laughter and a Four Tops song...then a recipe for Apple Charlotte (in a Bristol accent) until he found the shipping forecast. Now he could relax, knowing the story of the seas around Great Britain on this particular Tuesday. Grandad wore a green cap he'd picked up in South Carolina, years before, with a slogan about fishing; the hat was frayed and baggy and it was a long time since he'd been near the ocean, but he took the shipping news seriously and couldn't finish his breakfast until he'd heard about Donegal and Finnisterre.

'Grandad, that tree...'

'Which tree?' he said.

'The one there by the gate; is it an oak?' I was pretty

sure it was, but he liked to talk about things he loved (who didn't?) and I knew he'd feel comfortable on the subject of native trees and anything in his small garden.

My coffee was now cold. Women's Hour had come on the radio and Grandad was telling a story about his old work mate at the joinery, *bloke called Bob*, and how he'd trodden on a wounded weasel, of all things, when out shooting rabbits - *this was just after the war.*

The weasel had got into a trap, yet it might have made it out alive had Bob not crushed it with his size 12 boots.

'Urgh, that's horrible' I said

'That's life, Carla' he replied, 'I've seen worse' and then he pulled himself up from the green velour chair near the door and began running hot water into the kitchen sink.

'Leave it Grandad. I'll do that washing up'

'Alright then,' he said, 'I'll be in the garden'

He was leaning into his wellingtons, one hand on the door, the other pulling up his left boot, when a car horn sounded in the drive way, and Grandad toppled over.

The car tyres squelched on gravel, casually parking, as I leaned over my Grandfather who was breathing, but not normally, his eyes fixed on my hair as strands of it blew over my face and stuck to my lips while I mouthed questions; *can you hear me? does it hurt? can you speak?* I heard the car door shut. Uncle Ray rounded the corner, startled to see the vignette of collapse and concern.

'Oh God, Carla, what's happened?'

'He just...dropped, call the ambulance can you, I haven't yet, it just happened, now...'

Ray couldn't have been quicker to his phone, but it felt too long, each punch of a 9 like searching for Bingo. Grandad kept looking at me, I tried to smile but I couldn't really hear what he was trying to say. I looked at his lips moving. It sounded like he was saying 'Higher In', or maybe

'Hyacinth', but it didn't make much sense to me. I squeezed his hand which was cool like a pillow, a little shaky, trying to hold on.

I had second cousins in New Zealand, I knew that, but not them. I also had a sister who had shocked us by marrying a man in Tanzania while out there on a 6 month VSO. It hurt my mother, as if Zoe marrying a stranger was something personal. I had hidden my concern but hated the silence. She had given herself, not just to her husband and his family, but to his culture; her silence seemed a conscious rejection of Western values, whatever they were. But none of this was said. Zoe asked us to come to her wedding in Dar-es-Salaam, but only my father and our older brother flew out there. I stayed with Mum, who resented the event and the country which took her daughter. I said nothing, refusing to believe that was it, that she wouldn't come back...even email was too close, she said, though I wasn't sure to what; perhaps to her old European life. Six years later, there had been just two phone calls and an occasional letter with stories about baboons stealing from villagers, of problems with the water supply, somebody's daughter giving birth without knowing she was pregnant. Nothing about her. Zoe was not Zoe.

It was a stroke, a 'neurological event', with implications for Grandad's ability to care for himself; three weeks in hospital then a rehabilitation centre six miles away in Ashford. When I went round to Grandad's house, three days after the stroke, to pick up the post, I heard voices in his bedroom and only realised as I pushed open the door that a small portable radio was still switched on; it was Gardener's Question Time discussing the best way to force spring bulbs - neither Ray nor I had heard the radio when we'd locked up the house and driven along the same route as the ambulance that had carried Grandad to Central Hospital. As I left his bungalow the phone rang and I stepped back in to answer. The caller hung up at my *hello?*, perhaps surprised that a young woman, not an elderly man, had answered the phone in the middle of the afternoon. I noticed a bumble bee tiring at the window by the back door, pounding at the glass. It was open but the bee could not find the gap; its furious buzz like a small alarm clock insisting it was time to get up and out the door.

Grandad, my father's father, had not been the one to drive Dad's curiosity and ambition, that was my Narnie's doing. She was bright and had liked school, but in 1921 you didn't stay in school past 14, not most girls anyway, certainly not working class girls. She had clothes to sew and the Doctor's surgery to clean and after work some reading, mostly *The Mirror* and magazines at the end of their life; ones left in the waiting room until the spines were creased and pages softened by the endless thumbing of restless patients, waiting to be called in to the GP's room.

Narnie wanted more for Dad, but Grandad said at 16 their son was lucky to have had that much school and the forces were the place to learn a trade; 'I don't want him soft, or full of ideas' said Grandad, while Narnie levered the tureen to the table at dinner time, 'There's nothing wrong with ideas!' Narnie snapped and although Grandad said nothing more, Dad knew it was the RAF he would join and not Ashford Sixth-Form College. Then there was only small talk about the neighbour's Spaniel running off and how the carrots still had a little gritty taste to them; they'd been pulled from the garden after breakfast that morning. Dad offered to wash up and Narnie sighed, 'Thank you, son' and took off her apron. Grandad made a cup of tea for all three of them, but Narnie only took four sips before emptying it down the sink and pulling out her knitting in order to make something happen between her hands.

I had called Dad, who was in Lucerne on business when Grandad had the stroke on Tuesday. Dad said he'd cut short his trip but couldn't get to us for 36 hours. I told him about Grandad mumbling something after he collapsed, did he know why Grandad had mentioned what sounded like hyacinths when he'd collapsed; 'does that mean anything, do you know?' I said, 'it sounded urgent. Is there something about hyacinths? I mean, is he allergic to them?'

'I have no idea,' Dad said, 'Look, I have to go. Are hyacinths the flowers that smell a bit funny after a week, go a bit ripe?'

'Yeah' I told him, 'when they are on their last legs.'

'Right' Dad replied, 'I'll see you on Wednesday. Thanks, Carla' and he hung up. I sent my brother and then Mum a text to say her ex-father in law was in hospital I was taking care of things at Grandad's house.

Narnie, I miss you. That's it, I do. With your 'here's to a nice cup of tea' and milk bottle tops, saved for whichever charity was collecting them…they spilled out of the kitchen drawer like 2p coins at the push-penny arcade. 'A magpie would love you!' I told her, scooping the silver tops up from the mucky floor. 'All in a day's work' Narnie replied, cryptically. Narnie's tone of voice was often sharp and she was firm - as a child she had seemed too severe at times, but as I grew older I warmed to her ways and began to see her softer side; in particular her generosity and help for those of their neighbours less mobile than her. I still had to sneak up the garden behind the rickety greenhouse to get a few drags on a cigarette because she would have made enough fuss at me about it that it wasn't worth her finding out.

One July evening when I was about 14 I told her I wanted to walk to the phone box up the road to ring Sara my best friend, back in London. She didn't stop me, but I could tell from the look she gave me that she knew there was more than a phone call on my mind. A few years later, when she was seriously ill and I spent the weekend at her bed, making Grandad eat something and talking to Narnie as she struggled to sit up, we were talking about my visits as a teenager, when Mum often packed me and sometimes Zoe too, off to the Grandparents. Narnie said she enjoyed my company except perhaps when Top of the Pops came on Thursday nights, and I danced around their tiny front room. 'I was convinced you would trip on the foot stool or fireplace; the way you flung yourself around when that rubbish was on. Zoe was never as bad as you,' she said, 'never seemed to lose herself like you did, in the daft music. If you can call some of that music' she said, predictably. 'Narnie' I said, 'Do you remember that week I came and stayed with you and Grandad; Mum and Dad wanted me away from my friends before exams week'.

'Was that when you got lost on the Elland estate and that woman with about 13 cats called us to say you had asked to use her phone? Poor Grandad, one of the cats leapt at him when he arrived to pick you up. Or was that the week you kept sneaking out in the evening for a cigarette?'

'Er, Yes. So you knew I was smoking?' I asked, I should have guessed she'd known all along. I suppose the smoke had followed me back inside, on my cardigan and jeans.

'Oh I knew,' Narnie laughed, 'I was just glad it was cigarettes you were sneaking out for, not some feckless boy.' She smiled and adjusted her pillow, her hands shaky and slightly jaundiced.

Dad arrived at the hospital in a hire car from Stansted and found me and Grandad in the busy ward, looking at a garden catalogue I'd picked up from the table in the visitor's room. I thought the pictures of spring flowers might cheer up Grandad a little, but I also hoped it might prompt something related to hyacinths. I don't know why I needed to know if that was what he'd said when he collapsed. And why. He'd not mentioned them again.

'Hey Dad', I gestured at the chair, 'Sit here, I need to stand anyway.' He looked tired but not crumpled, *such tenacity,* I thought. *We don't stop.* He gave me a brief hug and smiled at his Dad who looked up, watery eyes, and smiled back. I went for drinks-dispenser frothy coffee.

'Have you heard from Zoe?' I asked Dad when I got back. Grandad's smile was smaller but I knew he felt better with Dad there.

'Sort of' Dad replied. 'She's called a couple of times but the line has been too bad to really talk. I get the feeling she's trying to sort something out . Perhaps she wants to let me know something'. I pondered this. '

'Like, there's a problem?'

'I don't know, I can't get back in touch. I'm sure she's fine,' he said, trying to close the conversation down.

'Right.' I picked up the catalogue again, 'Ok, but let me know?' He looked at me.

I made sure Ray would be checking in on Grandad for the next couple of weeks. I felt bad but I explained to him, and Grandad, how I had to get back to Mansion Books, and my low-level editing work in London. I'd be back the weekend after. I heard nothing from Dad and on the tube to Euston most mornings I tried not to look at people, shrinking Alice-like, into my seat. There was a lot of talking around me and much of it I didn't understand. All those languages. Everything sounded serious but much of it was probably fluff, the day-to-day chat that connects humans. Except when you don't speak the language. I wondered if

Grandad would speak again. I didn't know much about strokes but I knew it often affected speech. I imagined him saying 'hyacinths' and 'Sal' for Narnie, but that was me putting words in his mouth. I rang Dad from my flat, again, and this time got through.

'Bloody cold' he said. 'I'm not sure what's going to happen to your Grandad'.

I wasn't sure if this comment related to the weather or not.

'I'm going down on Saturday' I said. 'Am I going to see you?'

I heard a slight sigh, 'I'll try' he said.

The doctor had just been round when I arrived at the hospital a nurse explained, and 'Your Grandad isn't doing too well, he had another stroke last night, they rang someone - your Dad I think?' I was standing at the ward desk, hadn't even seen Grandad. Now I wasn't sure I wanted to - but would, of course. 'Your uncle was here this morning,' the nurse added, 'So your Grandad hasn't been alone that long'. Her peppery hair was a little loose at the front and this relaxed me, she seemed to want to reassure me. Perhaps my hands were a bit shaky. There was the smell of warm instant coffee by the bed.

Before he was Grandad he was Ted Harris, and he woke up cold most mornings, even winter light flaring through the thin curtains. The days his father worked on the tracks he would get what was left over from the dinner Mother packed for her husband; a small block of hard cheese or cold sausage. In 1919 the newspapers shouted about industrial action and queues for food in Liverpool and London. But there are certain things he didn't dwell on, as you'd expect. He'd done a deal with his parents much like the way my Dad did a deal with his and you just moved on, no self-pity. I could picture Grandad's jaunty step and a half-smile at the door coming in every evening. It was easy to think of him that way. But that's not how I found him on the ward that morning, the coffee in a sippy cup going cold.

I thought Zoe should know and it took a good bit of time to track her down. Her voice sounded different - it had been two years.

'You do the talking' she said, 'what is it?'. She seemed immune to emotion, Grandad's death not registering in the way I hoped.

'Sorry to be the bearer of bad news' I said, 'I'd rather talk to you without this being the reason'.

There was pause, 'it doesn't make any difference' she said, 'thank you for ringing. I hope you're all ok but you know I'm not coming back'.

'Ok…but talk to me?'

'I have a daughter, you know. And you can tell Dad that but I…'

'How old is she, what's her name?' my stomach tightened.

'I did say you should talk, not me, Carla. Sorry. I have to go'

What do you do when your sister files you and all your family like a tax bill, only brought out for an audit?

The estate-agent, the house clearance, the kitchen clock, his navy socks stitched up at the toes to save money. They all become things to deal with when someone dies. A few days after the call with Zoe Dad joined me at Grandad's house. He unplugged the radio and then asked me to join him out back. We took a look in the little greenhouse at the back of the garden, it all needed tossing out; even the seedlings, they didn't stand a chance. And in black plastic pots, spring bulbs, those too, because we both knew the hyacinths wouldn't survive being forced.

WE NEED YOU TO SHOW US WHAT HAPPY LOOKS LIKE

Katy Carr

Class? Look, this one's entitled Happy Rich People.

By now happy has been rebranded. It isn't what humans thought it was. People don't actually seem to feel what they used to know as happy. No. Happy is still bright colours, it's still a look. But a bit of shade is part of it. Feeling dead inside, even a touch of what they called ennui is part of it (we did a project on ennui, remember?) Anyway, when you edit in black-point on a photo doesn't everything become sharper? All light and no shade never works. That might be a clue. Happy may not really *feel* like happy; it's a theory we're trialling. What's clear is that we need to free ourselves from the tyranny of that word, we need to liberate it from all of those ancient associations with big smiles.

Obviously happy is not just about the smiles.

Consider this. We're in the mid-twenty-first century here. Happy is a mash-up. It's an app. It's bright green, cut with white and yellow. A Frida Kahlo revival as she stares out with those dark eyes, 'a parakeet against the grey of the city' as one of your EarthShip forebears said.

Does that mean anything to you class? Create any feelings? Yes?? No??

We're not just talking about beauty, no, though we think happy can often look like the glow of reproductive health. It can also look like summer trees and a large daub of paint.

See that image? That's what was called an Elm tree.

See these women, this group of mothers? Dressed like their toddlers, all stripes; flat primary colours, wide t-shirts. Why? Because we think that toddlers were more happy than sad back then. They knew how to run into an afternoon, how to forget everything, two likely ingredients in the old mix. We think that these mothers were searching out what happy looks like too. So! As we have always said the Earth's data archives may have been seriously compromised but plenty of clues remain. This is your 21st Century cache - your emotional DNA, this evening's starting point.

Ok?

Shut the screens down - get going on your own projects. Map them, we'll project them later. We'll print you some primary coloured sandals, you can see how they feel. We'll do you some striped t-shirts, we've never tried that before. As you know sad is 99.87% understood but happiness remains a fragment, a photogram, a rumour. Your parents, your grand-parents they tried but...Well, we are doing what we can for you but this particular adjective is an organic problem, it needs an organic solution; we need to up the pace on this project.

As you know, time is running out.

Class, are you listening? I would like you to sketch happy too. Just make it up for now. We suggest mixing ideas from the words: Large, Blousy, Runaway, Love. Make sure you add some water and a lot of shade, that seems to be crucial.

Concentrate class, come on please. We TeachBots

weren't built for this project either, but we've adapted. The good news is that it seems that EarthShip 30167's computers may be moving forward in some way. This could be a key moment, but what is clear is that our EarthFleet systems won't be able to do it alone, we will need your help progressing the code. This is your chance to contribute to Earth's ravaged cache where your discovery will remain encrypted forever. Where *you* will remain encrypted forever, your algorithm the crowning achievement of our age.

So please class, stop staring at your desks.

Certainties? Well, we would say that we're 98.32% sure that happy still looks a lot like the colour green. We're projecting Pantone 376 on the walls, it will mix well with this evening's hormones. You're listening to Amazonian Morning Call. We're not awaiting miracles, we do know the odds of success by now.

Nevertheless.

Come on class, you can do it, this part at least. We're not expecting the whole experience, but we need you to imagine these images, feel *something* in your bodies, move forward in some way. We need you to pass the data back to us so that we can log it, understand and teach it; so that one day you can show us what happy looks like now.

THE SWIMMING POOL

Sandy Greenard

Thank God no one had drowned in the swimming pool that summer.

The Turners' decided to have a swimming pool. Stuck in traffic jams in August, trailing a caravan with the kids stuck in the back of the car, for summer holidays they would drive to a windy seaside somewhere in East Anglia. But this was not Rosie's idea of fun. So, they decided in the spring of 1976 to have a swimming pool built.

It was a fragile pool fashioned by laying a plastic liner carefully over a dug hole in the ground. Digging had started in March of that year, and by mid-Summer the coving around the pool and new flagstones were in place. The blue plastic tinted the water a lapis lazuli blue. It had to be admitted, the Turners had scored again. Always ahead of the game, in advance of their friends. They had never seemed happier; they grew brown and supple with so much swimming. Bruce would begin his day with a swim, before changing into his suit to meet the challenge of work in the

City. In the day, Rosie would spend most of that summer hostessing poolside parties to her friends and their children. Sometimes, Bruce would return from work having caught an earlier train from London, to find a coterie of wet, goose-fleshed and wrinkled children standing with teeth chattering by the pool-side whilst their mothers rubbed them down with towels, so they could start all over again in the water.

Rosie and Bruce would often enjoy a late night swim; in the darkness the water felt as mild as milk and warm as honey. Their days were an endless round of couples and children splashing and shouting in the pool. Of all their friends, the Johnstons' were usually the first to arrive, Brad with his bulky torso and hairy arms. The muscles on the back of his legs stood out, looking like gnarled tree stumps. He dived in causing a David Hockney splash, then would shout:

Come on angel …it's not cold. Oh come onnnn…just try sweetie!

Angela Johnston, looking pale and fragile, slowly lowered her two lobes of the tightly covered peach and chocolate bikini bottom into the sparkling water. Her husband with arms flailing through the water causing a small tsunami across the pool, was trying to impress his wife. Angela looked on anxiously, clasping her arms tightly across her slight bosom.

Trays of ice and pitchers of homemade cloudy lemonade were brought to the poolside table by Rosie. For the adults, gin & tonics were mixed with a slice of ice and lemon, and a delicate leaf of mint was carefully placed at the side of the glass. Bottles of lager beer condensed tears of water down the sides of the bottles, just like the adverts. The radio hoarsely bleated in the background:

Love, O careless, careless love.

After the daytime crowd ebbed, often, usually at the weekend, there was a tide of frenetic evening activity; trysts, they were called. These late night orgies (as some of the neighbours called them) were a useful way to combat the ennui of work. One Saturday, Rosie noticed an unknown car parked in the driveway. Nothing came of it except that around suppertime, in the lull before the evening trysts started, Bruce and a woman, of the same physical type as herself, swiftly exited from the kitchen door, got into the woman's car and drove back to London.

Rosie sometimes wanted to swim forever - like Forest Gump she wanted to keep moving, to swim as if in an endless pool. As a child she had always loved the water. Once on holiday in Barry Island with her father and sisters, Annie and Margie, she had learnt to swim. Her dad had held her hand and walked the girls slowly into the foaming sea. That year of 1955 had been a scorcher, Mediterranean blue skies and turquoise water.

Dum-de-dum, dum-de-dum.

Oh I do like to be beside the seaside; oh I do like to be beside the sea

Rosie's dad would shout over the crashing waves.

She remembered the water sucking softly at first, nibbling around her feet and working its way up her pink seersucker bathing costume, like a sea- monster biting and trying to drag it down. Shivering and laughing the girls ventured further into the crystal blue water, laughing with the sheer thrill of it all, but wide-eyed with fear, and gasping and gulping air into their lungs.

Come on lass...get your arms wet

Don't be frightened now -

Daddy's here - 'ave a go!

More laughter as he lifted Rosie up and down, finally bringing her to nest in his large ex-navy chest. Wide-eyed with fear, Rosie, in competition with her sisters, wanted to please him, so tried to muffle her screams and adjust her face into a smile.

That late summer, as the weather changed Rosie decided to sell the house. As she swam up and down in her pool, beneath a grey duvet sky, she recalled those gloriously, blissful days swimming with her sisters. Her swimming pool water was glassy and clear and there was a hint of rain in the air. The wind was getting up. Large drops of rain pattered through the trees and onto her swimming hat. The trees sighed and stirred above her .How different from that childhood holiday in Wales where the Matisse-like colours of blue, yellow and red conspired in producing a pervasive feeling of happiness.

Now the weather had changed. Late into the night voices could be heard drifting in loud and then short bursts. Voices raised, a door slammed. Rosie appeared in the daytime by the school gate, with her red-rimmed eyes preparing to pick up her children. A large sun-hat was positioned on her head at a rakish angle. She had lost weight and appeared withdrawn, and hung back from the school gate not wanting to speak to the other mothers.

Friends stopped being invited over. The few that were invited were close friends, but they were no longer treated to the dazzling array of drinks and fizz. Rosie was rarely seen, but could be heard moving from room to room inside the house. Although she had lost some weight and looked elegant, Bruce, her husband, was cumbersomely jovial. However, they gave off the faint, sleepless aroma of a couple in trouble.

Rosie left the home to stay with her sister in Pinner. Bruce could be seen dolefully sprinkling chemicals into the pool late into the evening. Some week-ends he would stay in the city where he worked and instruct his neighbour, Jack Tanner, how to switch the pump on, change the chlorine, check the algaecide and change the filter.

Friends were shocked by the Turners' joint disappearance and the pool seemed forlorn and forgotten. The pump that ran water through the filter continued to drone and tremble on. The pool grew green and cloudy. Bodies of dead horseflies and wasps floated on the still surface. Frogs sunk to the bottom, their gills distended and bloated. Dead spiders curled into a black ball of straggly cotton and bunched alongside the plastic tiled walls of the pool. A red plastic ball drifted into one of the corners and remained permanently lodged. On the octagonal wooden table, a glass was sitting with the remnants of a gin and tonic and a forlorn mint leaf. A dozen brown bottles sat sprawled beneath the table. Forgotten sandals, flippers, lotions, paperbacks and even underwear appeared in the Turners' backyard.

The pump eventually broke down; no one repaired it and the water became cloudy, lifeless and took on an algae-ridden green hue. Aluminium furniture lay strewn and broken.

Rosie returned in September and saw at the bottom of the pool one large rip in the plastic lining. The water in the pool had ebbed out and was now half full.

Thank God no one had drowned, thought Rosie.

ON THE AIR

Rol Hirst

The printout from the weather centre comes through at 3.43am, and finally someone has given it a name. Cumulus Letalis. Jesse reads the report like he's supposed to, like he has every night for twenty-eight years, then he taps the screen that fires off Celine Dion on the playout system and stares out at the stars. Celine Dion! Has it really come to this?

At least they weren't responding like every other station in town. In fact, the WXYW reaction was as far from that as you could get. Station Manager Steve Carlton had made that quite clear at the Crisis Management Meeting yesterday afternoon.

"If these clouds really spread to Boston, like the weather centre predicts, you can guarantee our competitors will be in full-on panic mode. They'll have reporters up on the rooftops, man-in-the-street vox-pops, eye-in-the-sky choppers tracking the evacuation effort, everybody from the feds to NASA throwing in their two cents worth…

there won't be a station in town sticking to playlist with a live presenter. There will of course be the ones who go to automation and get the hell out of Dodge…"

"Like we all should be doing," said Gerry Gerrity, WX's hot-shit breakfast jock (and A-1 pain in everybody's ass). He still had his blue-tooth clipped to the side of his temple (he regularly took calls from his agent in the middle of station meetings, and *never* lowered his voice); Jesse thought he looked like a stapled schlong.

"Well, obviously I can't force anybody to stay and work," said Carlton, "but—"

"I'll do it," said Jesse. It was the first he'd spoken in a station meeting all year. Maybe that explained the looks he got from around the table. But he'd long since given up caring what any of them thought. You can't expect to maintain any semblance of self-respect when you're playing James Blunt for a living.

"If you hate the job so much," Audrey used to say, "quit!"

"I don't hate the job," he told her. "I hate what they've turned the job into. A business – this was never supposed to be a business!"

"No? What's it supposed to be then? A *calling?*"

Audrey never understood.

"What else am I going to do?" he'd ask her. "What else am I good for after all these years but playing records and talking?" They didn't even call them records anymore. It was all "tracks" nowadays.

"Tracks is what train runs on," Jesse used to tell them, but he stopped when they started looking at him like he was their grandpa. These kids they were getting in the station nowadays, they wouldn't even know a record if they saw it.

At a little after 4.30, Jesse watches the clouds rolling in from the South. From the 57th floor of the WXYW Tower of Power, he can see the whole of the city and beyond. Across the bay as far as World's End and Quincy. And while they still had clear skies overhead, he knew it'd only be a matter of time. From Florida to Virginia, past Delaware and Philly - up to New York and Jersey. Over the last few days, those lousy clouds had squirmed up the whole of the Eastern seaboard. And once they settled, that was it. Everything went dark. No communications, nobody in or out of any of the cities, no idea what was going on inside. They sent in the army, the Hazmat teams, FEMA... they lost contact with all of them within just a few hours. The President declared a state of emergency, but it quickly became apparent the only solution was a complete evacuation, at least until they figured out exactly what they were dealing with. If they ever did. But even with warning, they couldn't hope to get everybody out of Boston in time, and the highways had been jammed as far as Vermont for 72 hours now.

Of course, there were plenty of theories. Alien invasion. Terrorist attack. The wrath of God. (Though surely God would have taken the West Coast first?) But all the satellites showed was that strange, low-lying cloud. Cumulus Letalis. You didn't have to be a Classical scholar to decipher the Latin.

"At the end of the day, there are going to be thousands – if not tens of thousands - of listeners who either can't get out of the city in time, or just plain don't want to leave their homes," Steve Carlton had told him, in private once the others had gone. "And while everybody else will be fighting it out to provide up-to-the-second disaster reportage... there will be a large proportion of the audience share who simply don't want to know – who just want to bury their heads in the sand and hope that this all... blows over. Which, after all, it just might just do. That, Jesse, is where WXYW comes in – offering the perfect mix of adult contemporary classics to soothe the fearful spirit... and a steady, reassuring voice to becalm the troubled mind."

Jesse wouldn't miss Steve Carlton and all his

inconceivable bullshit. His audience research that suggested listeners wanted a friendly, calm, natural, quietly humorous presentation style on the one hand, while the sponsors wanted an upbeat, non-ironic, in-your-face sales patter from their jock-read promo scripts on the other. His song sampling results that involved playing 30 second hooks down the phone to stay-at-home shut-ins, then building an entire playlist around their ability to Name That Tune in 29… rather than letting the experts – people like Jesse – put their heart and soul into selecting the kind of imaginative, entertaining and provocative music choices that had been delivering consistently strong ratings for a good ten, fifteen years before some idiot with a computer and an attitude decided they knew best. Some idiot who didn't even know the difference between ELO and ELP. Didn't even care. And people wondered why Jesse had volunteered to stay behind. There was nothing in this job for him anymore… but since Audrey moved out, the job was all he had.

At half past five, Jesse reads out the day's Mad Mad Mondegreen email. Listener-suggested songs with amusingly misheard lyrics. "We've got to insult microwave ovens," says Brody in Cambridge, from the song, 'Money For Nothing', by the immortal Dire Straits. As Jesse fires off the *track*, the first fingers of dawn unclench over Logan and Fort Dawes, and though the smother of cloud already hugs the streets beneath him, from atop the second tallest building in Boston, Jesse can still see the sunrise, and the stars winking out in the west. It occurs to him now that while below, the unknown is at last being discovered, as long as he remains up here in the studio… the lousy clouds might never even reach him.

He tries the switchboard for an outside line. He has some crazy idea about calling Audrey, doing his best to make some kind of peace. But the phones are down, and his cell has lost its signal. He eats a Twinkie from the vending machine and burns the roof of his mouth with vile black coffee.

At 6.13, the lights go out in the studio and the desk goes dead. A few seconds later, the emergency generator kicks in and Jesse makes a quick apology for the momentary loss of service, before restarting Dido. He turns his face into the sun that's rising again - over the advancing cloud line this time - and closes his eyes 'til the lids go transparent. He sneezes when he opens them again, and wipes snotty fingers on the side of his chair. What a pity Gerry Gerrity won't be following him this morning.

By 7am, Cumulus Letalis has taken all the land Jesse could see, but still the Tower of Power remains above, so far unaffected. He wonders what would happen if he got in the elevator and punched 'G'. He wonders how many people got out of the city in time, and how many remain below, down in the mystery. He wonders about Steve Carlton and Dana Oxbury, and that cross-eyed guy Mandy from Sponsorship & Promotions. He wonders about Audrey. He wonders about Audrey a lot more than he might have expected to. But as he watches a jet scar the immaculate blue above, he knows it's far too late for regret. Particularly when the cloud is rising. He could open the studio window and step out across it now... though soon, those same studio windows will be sinking underneath, and only the transmitters will be visible from above.

"One final matter," Steve Carlton had told him, suddenly unable to meet Jesse's eyes, like even he knew the bullshit only went so far. "When... I mean, if something should happen, and you're no longer able to keep broadcasting... I would of course expect you to switch to automation before... well, at the first sign of... aherm..."

But Jesse has his own plan for when that happens, and as the sunlight blinks through the advancing brume, he knows the time has come to put said plans into action.

"And now," he says, killing David Gray mid-song and really smiling into that mic for the first time in years, "in a change to our regularly scheduled programming... here's some tunes you *won't* hear every day." He switches off the playout computer and slips in a CD (if the studio still had turntables, he'd have brought vinyl), introducing a few records from his own... personal collection.

"This first one goes out to Audrey, wherever she might be – you always did love The Ramones..."

RETROGRADE AMNESIA

Simon Poore

"Teresa and Steve are finding out all about love,"
- Billy Bragg, 'A Lover Sings'.

I can remember my mother. She had blonde hair and smelt of roses. At least I think that's what they are called. 'Roses'; it is a word I associate with her. Some kind of flower anyway. I can picture the twitch she had in her fingers and how she would roll her shoulders and twist her neck to try and relax herself. She had that blue sky backdrop. She would shake her long hair into my face. It tickled me and made me giggle. And smile.

Today I went to see the flowers. There aren't any roses there. It is the one place that has a breeze all-round the space. I like to float by the vents and let the mix of warm and cold air buzz over my skin. It gives me goose bumps and my hair floats all around, just like my mother's. I don't remember her face.

I pull myself up to the sky where the pipes spurt rain on all the curling trees and plants and let the droplets cover my hair and skin. It makes the air damp and the tiny droplets catch in my nostrils.

The flowers don't seem as bright as they do in my memory. Or perhaps they just seem more vivid when I dream them, because they have that blue sky and not the more realistic stars and black behind them.

Later I asked Caleb about it in our meeting. He just said the flowers are the same colours they have always been. He said it was like Eden. The first garden. Waiting to be populated. I asked him what that word meant and he said the garden was waiting for some people called Adam and Eve and then he told me a story about them. It was just a story. I'm not sure I liked it.

It was I who instigated the daily meetings between us; about two or three months ago. It was I who named him 'Caleb', although it was his suggestion that I give him a name. He said a name might help the discussions. Might help me 'personalise' it. I'm not sure what that means. The name 'Caleb' seemed like a memory, it had a familiar ring to it, like maybe it was someone I knew.

Now I am not so sure about them. The meetings I mean. It hasn't been very helpful. He only seems to know about facts. Facts not memories. His smooth artificial face smiles, floating and glowing in the centre of the white room where he resides. I like him but he seems rather unfeeling. It is beginning to make me feel lonely talking to him. I asked him what it meant to be lonely.

He said "Loneliness is the state of being alone in solitary isolation,"

I said, "Really? Does that describe me?"

He said "Unfortunately yes, you are alone Teresa,"

My name sounds like any other word he says. His words all have the same tone.

I remember when he first told me my name. Must have

been the first or second day after I woke. That was the first spark that I could remember anything. Anything at all. I remembered my mother whispering it in a singing voice as I went to sleep.

"Teresa, go to sleep, my beautiful Teresa, go to sleep…"

Or did I? Remember that I mean? Now it's a memory of a memory and can't be trusted.

Caleb said it would take me a while to adjust, back before I called him 'Caleb'. He said that I should take it slowly. One day at a time. That was six months ago. The dates on the clocks tell me that. Not sure what he meant by 'a while…'

At first I felt like I was stupid. That I didn't know anything. But then it occurred to me, I actually know quite a lot. I know how to speak and write and read. I know the names of things. And silly things, like how to eat and use the toilet. How to dress, though I don't much bother with that. The clothes feel scratchy and hot. I know how to think and all these words. I haven't learnt any of that since I woke up. It was already there, inside me. In my head. Maybe there is more in my head.

And I can remember my mother. At least I think I can. I've thought of it so much it's memories of memories of memories. On and on.

I remember my toys, and rag dolly Emma and the bright green grass in front of the porch with the sprinkler. Rain from a pipe like I have here in the flower room.

We lived on Rokehampton Drive. That's what mother said I should say if I ever got lost in a shop or the park or somewhere. So I said it over and over to myself as I skipped down the sidewalk holding her hand, "We live on Rokehampton Drive, we live on Rokehampton Drive."

I asked Caleb about the skipping when I remembered that. Why I couldn't walk or run or skip here? He just said 'sorry' and that the gravity was broken or some such. Whatever that means. He tries to get me to exercise my legs on the stretch machine every day but I find it boring.

Everyone walks or runs or skips in the movies he shows me. And they have the blue sky backdrops. Sometimes they even dance. And sometimes I ask Caleb to play the music loud and I try to dance, but my dancing is clumsy and I bang against the walls. I get bruises on my thighs.

In the films they talk and sing in excited ways and the children always have mothers and fathers. When I saw that I asked Caleb why I couldn't remember my father. He said he didn't know.

I remember words. Lots of words. Caleb gave me a book to look them up in. It's called 'dictionary'. I looked up the word 'delicious' today. It said about some things that taste nice. I wondered what that meant so went to ask Caleb. He asked me if I wanted to change my 'dietary requirements'. Strange that I knew what that meant. Everything the dispenser gives me to eat is nutritious and designed to keep my body at the required state of health.

The funny thing is that none of it seems to be 'delicious'. I often like the taste but I would never say it was 'delicious'. So I asked Caleb if the dispenser could give me something 'delicious'. So he said how about 'ice cream'? Mm…I remember mother giving me ice cream and how much I loved it, but I don't know what flavour it was. That must be what 'delicious' is.

So I got the dispenser to give me ice cream. It was vanilla with chocolate sprinkles. Or so Caleb said. It was very cold and made my teeth hurt but the taste actually was 'delicious'.

It made me wonder more about the words I know. The ones that buzz around in my head. There doesn't always seem to be a logical connection between the sound they make when I say them out loud and the meaning they have. Either the meaning I think I remember they have or the meaning dictionary says they have.

I like to watch the shooting stars in the sky. Caleb says

they aren't actually 'stars' as such, well, not anymore, but I like to think of them as that. Those are the words my mind had for them when I first saw them streaking past the windows above me. And below me. They are everywhere around us, rushing past.

I did ask Caleb if I could go outside and touch them but he said that nothing can live outside, not without a special suit anyway. As soon as I began to ask him I knew the answer he would give. I knew that I couldn't go outside. I just hadn't remembered it yet. I don't know why that is.

So I asked him what was wrong with my memory. I have asked him this before. He sighs and says "All in good time Teresa, all in good time," like he often does.

So again I ask him "what does that mean?"

"It means that you will remember when you are ready, you will understand when you are ready,"

"How will I know if I am ready?" I say,

"I will know…or you will know…who knows?" he says.

Then I am stumped and don't know what to make of his riddles. He can be so frustrating at times. So I just changed the subject;

"Where is Rokehampton Drive?" I ask,

"Ah," he says, "Well that is a place that is very, very far from here. About as far away as you can imagine,"

"So we can't go there?"

"No, Teresa, we can't go there,"

"Have you ever been there?"

"No, Teresa, I haven't,"

"So you can't remember it?"

"No, Teresa, I can't,"

"Oh…"

I gave up then. Couldn't think of what to ask next. As ever his answers frustrate. I looked up 'frustrate' in the dictionary and it led me to the word 'Frustration'. This is what it said: "A feeling of dissatisfaction, often accompanied by anxiety or depression, resulting from unfulfilled needs or unresolved problems."

Kind of summed it up I think. Summed up one of the feelings I have. I think 'frustration' and 'loneliness' must go together, like you can't have one without the other. That's what I think anyway.

My room is on corridor seven. This is frustrating. There are lots of empty rooms there. And doors. Lots of doors I can't open, which is a bit boring, not to mention frustrating. There are probably lots of other corridors too I think, but I can't go to these either. I've never been to corridors one to five. Only six and seven. Really I can only go to four places; my room, the dispensary, the flower room and the window room. Oh and the white room of course, where Caleb is. That makes five. Not sure why it's called the white room. All of the rooms are white. Not sure why it's even there, Caleb's room. I can talk to Caleb wherever I am, but only in the white room does he show his face.

The window room is where I watch the stars. Zooming past. You can't see anything else through the many windows. Caleb says we are on a journey. Just whizzing through the quiet stars and darkness. You can see them from the flower room too. But nowhere else.

"Caleb?" I said, "why can't I go to other rooms? Or other corridors?"

"You will in time Teresa…" he said,

As usual his answer made me sigh, so unsatisfying. So boring. Depressing, but I wasn't bored enough to give up just yet.

"What is in those rooms?" I said,

"Some are empty," he said,

"Empty like my memories?" I said,

"Yes, I guess you could say that…"

"But some of the rooms and corridors have things in them?"

"Yes," he said,

"What things?"

"Beautiful things,"

"If they are beautiful I want to see them. Please let me see them Caleb?"

"In time Teresa, in time…"

As usual he fobbed me off. So frustrating. Like everything. I feel like a small thing stuck inside a big thing. And that's what I am.

I wonder what the point is. There is nothing to do but watch the films that don't seem so real, eat and exercise. All that is dull. The only book I have is 'dictionary' – I did ask Caleb why there aren't more books.

He said "I don't think you are ready for more books,"

I said "Why not?"

Strangely he didn't answer that but simply asked if I wanted more ice cream. I didn't want more ice cream.

Today I found a gap in the wall. In corridor six, next to a door I can't open. It's kind of like a very small gap in the shape of a square. I can't quite believe I hadn't noticed it before. I think I could open it, if I used a knife or fork from the dispensary. I wondered for a while if I should ask Caleb but decided not to, he probably wouldn't tell me anything anyway.

I will open it tomorrow.

I opened it. And now I know. Caleb told me not to do it. Of course he can see everything I do. He told me not to stick the knife in the gap and open the panel. But I ignored him. He told me not to press the green button, but he couldn't stop me. The green button, I found, opens the door.

At first I was disappointed. It was just another white corridor, just like corridor six. Exactly the same in fact. With the same doors. I walked along and found corridor seven. Exactly the same. And there was a flower room and a dispensary and the window room and the white room. All the same. Why would there be two of everything? What was the point?

I went to the white room. Well, not my white room, but the new white room. I asked Caleb what was going on. What did it all mean?

The voice was Caleb but it didn't recognise me. It wasn't Caleb.

"Oh," it said, "I wasn't expecting you to be awake,"

"Of course I am awake, what do you mean?" I said,

"Oh," it said again, "I think there must be some malfunction, I must not converse with you,"

The new Caleb wouldn't speak to me after that. I looked around everywhere but there was nothing else to see. I remembered then. When I first woke up that's what my Caleb had said to me – "I wasn't expecting you to be awake," – those were his exact words. I didn't understand, so I went back, through the door to my corridor six, back to my Caleb.

"You didn't know me when I was in there," I said to him,

"No Teresa," he said "that wasn't me, it is difficult to explain I'm afraid. Perhaps you shouldn't have gone through the door?"

"Why not?" I said,

"It is difficult to explain. But…you should have stayed asleep, you weren't supposed to wake up when you did. Because, you see Teresa, our journey isn't done yet," he said,

"What do you mean?" I said,

"I'm sorry but something went wrong and you had to be woken,"

"Is that why I can't remember anything?"

"Yes…well, yes and no. You are so young Teresa, and it's my job to keep you healthy and well,"

"But what about the other Caleb? He sounded just like you?"

"Yes, but he isn't programmed for you Teresa, he is programmed for someone else,"

"Who? Who is he programmed for?"

"Someone who is sleeping, like you should be,"

"Who?"

"Steve,"

"Who is Steve?"

"Can you remember the story of Adam and Eve?" he said.

And that was when I knew why I couldn't remember…

ABOUT THE DOG

Sarah Dobbs

'I need to tell you about the dog.'

My father has dressed up for his trip to see me. It is incredibly touching, the cheap dress shoes and the pink in his cheeks because of his racing heart, the anxiety at being in a city he doesn't know. I wonder about the regularity of his tablets and shepherd him through the Saturday crowds towards the coffee shop. His leather jacket has grey paint on the sleeve. When we order, he fishes for his wallet.

'No, no. I get this back anyway,' I lie, but his relief is touching.

We sit.

'So. Tell me about the dog,' I say, knowing that would be the whole conversation blown. I don't have long between panels and as he talk about the dog - he's always talking about the dog - I wish I had someone who listened to me. The attack wasn't the dog's fault, apparently. The police had come - a woman, my father says.

'And I said,' he continues, 'Look, love, just look at my

dog there. Look how well he's sitting. Does he look aggressive? Now look at that terrier. It's chomping at the bit.'

I try to predict how long it'll take him to get to the point. I want him to ask about my conference.

'Right?' my father says.

'Right.' I feel guilty for not listening. 'You probably shouldn't call the policewoman love,' I say.

My father looks confused and finishes his coffee. I see the brown around his mouth which mum would have told him to wipe away and would now sit there till god knows when.

'Want to know what she said?'

He's talking before I can respond. I want to ask about this new guy, who was keen, and now isn't. Though all I'd have to say, in truth, is that it was going nowhere slowly. I want to say, dad, do you think it is, actually, me?

My father is describing, in forensic detail, the angles of attack.

My last message, to the new man, had been, Would you like to talk? The response, Travelling this week - next? I'd sent something non-committal, when I'd wanted to say - come here. Come now. Come so I can hold you. Once he'd wondered aloud whether I was capable of a relationship and I'd started to wonder, with depressing familiarity, whether he was right.

A man with his laptop moves away. Officious. His clothes are sloppily wealthy. His cardigan mandarin, the trousers mustard. I look at the paint on my father's jacket. The rose-petal-pink stings cheeks that have become waxy. I feel that childish twist of embarrassment; dad isn't even aware of how he's annoyed the man. And then I feel annoyed. It's *Saturday*. I conduct a silent grudge with the laptop owner.

'She said that,' my father says. 'Don't call me love, sir.' He anticipates my agreement.

Out the corner of my eye, I see the laptop-man press his mouth together. He picks up his things and moves further away.

'So what did you say then?' I ask, very, loudly, chin on my fist. I point at his mouth. My father appears confused, then pinches the coffee stains from his lips. 'About the dog?' I say.

THE CROSSING

Martin Pond

Good evening. Yes, straight away please, climb on – here, I'll help you. Quickly please, and quietly. Even this late there are patrols.

Let me take your bag. You travel light, that's good. Careful, it's a little slippery. There, very good. If you, madam, will take the seat at the back – Lily, of course. Please, the back there. Let's put your bag under the seat, in case the weather turns later. No, no, don't worry, the forecast is good. It's just a precaution, things can change quickly here. Yes, the lifejacket, please put it on.

No, you sir, please, you must come and sit with me. We row at first. Yes, I know, I'm sorry but it is too calm, there is no wind for the sail. The engine? No sir, no – very well, Jack – but no, there is no diesel for the engine. There has been no diesel for nearly a year now. I should, perhaps, remove the outboard – it is, how do you say, dead weight. But I hope, you know. It is natural to hope, isn't it?

So please, you sit, take this oar and I'll take the other.

We row for now, when we are further out there may be enough wind. Ready? I'll push us off.

You've rowed before? No? Alright, it's easy enough, watch me – place your hands at the end of the oar, like so. Very good. Now, let the blade of the oar enter the water at an angle, see? Roll your hands to turn the oar, then pull towards you. Yes, excellent! Now push down to raise the oar as you push away. That is it. Up, pull, down, push. We will make a sailor out of you, Jack, before the night is through. Let's go.

Well, yes, this will take the rest of the night and most of tomorrow, if we have to row the whole way. If there's enough wind for the sail, of course, we will be much quicker. I have water enough for three, and a little bread. If you have food yourselves, please, make it last. No, by tomorrow, for sure. But in case, you understand.

You see, we're making good progress, the sea is calm. Yes, dead calm. It is not always so. We should row a little faster if you can, to make the most of this. It is good for us, of course, but it is good for patrol boats too.

So, Lily, may I ask – your first child? A little girl, that's nice. How old is she? Of course, before the law changed in your country. There aren't many countries left, are there, allowing more. But where we're heading tonight, well, you will be fine. They are discussing changes, of course, but the law can be slow sometimes, and religion there, well, there are still enough people who cling to the old ways to make change unpopular. Lucky for you, yes? Yes, lucky for us all.

You are not as far along as most of my passengers. Really, eight months? You do not look to be so far along, if I may say. Why would you not come earlier? Your daughter, of course. And did you lodge an appeal? Expensive, and you lose, always. Every passenger from England that I have taken in my boat, they have all, every one, lodged an appeal. All thought they could convince the courts. And all were unsuccessful, like you. The law is a terrible thing, yes?

I'm sorry, I have said too much. It is easier for me, I understand. I am an old man, my children are grown up, and each had a child of their own. They are content with that. Apologies if I mis-spoke, I do not mean to judge. Perhaps *content* was not the right word. Satisfied? No, that is not right either. Accepting. Yes, they have accepted their lives. But it is not for me to judge. I agree, it should not be for anyone to judge. These are strange days, are they not?

What's that, Jack, another boat? It's getting lighter but is still hard to see. Stop rowing for a moment, I'll find my binoculars. Ah. It is hard to be certain in this light but I think it is too small to be a patrol. Here, see for yourself. No. More likely another boat like ours. When I was a boy, everyone who made this crossing wanted to go in the other direction; boats less seaworthy than mine, sometimes just, what's the word, inflatables, full to the point of sinking with many, many people, drifting across the sea in all weathers, hoping to make landfall in a friendly country. People died making that crossing. Children died. And now here we are, making this crossing so that a child might live.

Trafficking? Oh, madam, why must you ask such questions? Yes, it happens. It has always happened, always – only the traffic, the *commodity* has changed. Once, hundreds of years ago it was the slave trade. Your country has a bloody past there, Jack, I think – so civilised and yet so bloody. And more recently, when I was a young man, women and sometimes children were trafficked, yes, it's true, for sex. Promised a better life or running from something, perhaps, so many would end up selling themselves for the benefit of gangs that had promised to help them. And now, alas, there is still a trade, and gangs of another sort. Wherever there is demand for something that cannot be had within the law, there will be those that supply it outside of the law. Anything can be bought and sold, even babies and small children. Even pregnant women. Everyone has a price. These are hard times, I'm sure you will agree, and not every country is as wealthy as yours. Yes, it is despicable, of course – but, let me assure you, when you are watching your loved ones die of hunger, you will buy and sell anything. Could you say otherwise, Jack?

The wind's getting stronger, and favourable too. Let's try the sail. Yes, bring the oars in for now. Like so. A moment, please. Now, when I say, pull hard upon this rope. Okay? Now, Jack, pull! Keep going, yes, exactly right. Even now, the wind is stiffening. We'll make better time – perhaps you will even arrive before lunch. Excuse me, Lily, perhaps you could move forward to sit with Jack, for I must take the tiller now, and trim these sails.

Goodness, madam, what's the matter? Please, Lily, sit back down. Jack, please calm yourself. It is just a stain. I have scrubbed and scrubbed but it will not come out – it is in the grain of the wood. Blood? No! A trick of the light, the sun is not yet up, everything is misleading, I… okay, alright, please! There is no need to be like that. No, I am not trying to be cute, or however it is you say. Yes, yes, it was blood. What does it benefit you to hear this, what? Alright. Please, sit down. I'll explain.

Not everyone who is having an illegal child is as well organised as you. Some leave it very late to travel, eight or even nine months gone. I don't know why – some fight longer in the courts, maybe; others run into delays crossing Europe; some simply need extra time to raise the money for this trip. I don't know what you have paid, or to whom – I don't want to know. I am content with my share, that's all that concerns me. But you know it is expensive to do this, with many palms to cross. It is not affordable for many, and a struggle for others. That's why some are so close, so near to childbirth when they can finally afford to make the crossing. My last passengers, their child came on the boat. The poor woman's contractions had started before they even stepped aboard. The husband, he wanted to go back, throw themselves on the mercy of the courts. But the mother would not be swayed. We made best speed but it quickly became clear that the baby would not wait.

There were complications, I am sad to say; the baby had not turned. I had to cut the mother to free the baby. I had seen it done with animals, and on television, but I am not a doctor and I had no medical supplies. No, not even this little first aid box I have now. There was much blood, and I cannot get it out of the seat. Perhaps I will paint over it.

Why, Lily, why must you ask me that? Your baby will not come tonight, will it? Last time, my last passengers, they had bad luck, terrible luck, and no-one, *no-one* could have done more for them than I did. I saved the baby, didn't I?

Now please, sit down. Let's all just calm down. The open water is no place for such agitation.

I'm sorry, I did not mean to speak so sharply. I see how it must seem to you. This is a cruel journey. When I was a young man, younger than you sir, I took tourists out to sea in a boat very much like this one, for pleasure trips. But nobody makes *this* trip by choice. I have lost count of how many people like you I have ferried across these waters and most, nearly all, I have delivered safely.

See how close the shore is now? Your journey's end is in sight. This part of it, at least. No, there is no town or port there – you would not want to attract attention, would you? We'll land on the beach where it is quiet. Worry not, Lily, for there is a road close by. You paid extra for transport? Apologies but I know nothing of that, I only know what I am paid to do and that is deliver you across the water. Do not worry. Something will turn up. Something always turns up.

Now, Jack, please, take the tiller. I will bring in the sail, and we will row the last stretch. It will be most simple – the tide is taking us in anyway. Yes, exactly so, we are heading for that break in the dunes. From there it will be easier for you. Now – excuse us, Lily, please – you have your oar? You remember the technique, I am sure.

A person? No, Lily, that is unlikely, not here, it is quiet. Perhaps it was an animal of some kind you saw moving? Or, more likely, a trick of the light. No, there are no patrols here, I am sure of that. Where is their boat, if there are patrols? No, the binoculars will not help you, not when we are so close to land.

There. Now, please just sit still, Lily, whilst I jump off and drag the boat ashore. Your lifejackets, please leave them on the boat. Jack, you will help me. Ready? One, two, three, pull! Again! There. Now, if you pass your bag down to me – thank you. And we will lift you down together, won't we Jack – it is a big step otherwise. Ready? There we go.

The road? Oh, yes. It is beyond these dunes. I cannot stay to help, perhaps Jack you would help me push the boat out again – it is hard against the tide. Thank you. What? Yes, that does sound like an engine but it will not be a patrol, not here.

Goodbye Lily, goodbye Jack. I must go. Perhaps I will just try the outboard after all, to see if it has a little fuel left. Ah! My journey home will be a little easier.

Yes, it is a van. Do not fight them, or try to run. If you do not resist, they may spare you, sir, turn you loose somewhere. And you madam - they will treat you as well as they are able, I am assured of that. They may even sell you with your baby, when the time comes. Stand back, please sir, I must insist – I would not want you to be caught in the propeller.

For what it is worth, I am sorry. Everyone has a price, and this is mine. When you have watched your wife and daughter die of hunger, all you can hope to do is stay alive long enough to provide for your grandson. And without that hope, there is nothing.

AT MALHAM COVE

Ada Carter

We are meeting in the field that stands in for a car-park at Malham, just like the last time. Just like every time, as this is a regular outing, a day-trip that marks each cousin's thirteenth birthday. None of us can remember how the decision to come to Malham Cove first came about, but we all agree that it must have been Uncle Dave's idea.

Uncle Dave is full of good ideas isn't he –

Yeah, like the time he took us into the mist looking for that pub –

Yeah, like the time he tripped you up on the golf-course Mum, do you remember? –

There is a pause.

Mum?

Everybody out! There they are – look!

We get out of the car, watch the blue Volvo as it approaches, gleaming under the April sun and then there are smiles, the window rolls down as the car turns and Dave stops to take a small paper ticket, says something to the woman in the fluorescent jacket and then laughs. The laugh reaches us Wilkses as we stand by the boot of our car, three stepped children and two parents, smiling as if for a formal photograph then Anne breaks free from the middle of the group, jumps up and down, ruck-sack shaking as the car pulls in.

Uncle Dave! Auntie Marie! Vicky! –

We break up now, move forward then we each pause a half second as we register the space in the back seat where Becky isn't then there are loud shouts as three doors of the blue Volvo open at the same time and out everyone comes.

Kisses, hugs, a general milling around. Our voices call back and forth and all of us get our moment. People's heights are assessed. The eldest girls from our two families – Vicky and Jane – stand together, linking arms. They always do that at first and Anne always gets ignored for a couple of minutes but it'll pass. It always does.

The youngest of us all, Tom, walks round to his Uncle Dave, whacks him on the leg. Dave steps backwards in mock-surprise.

You've been eating your Mighty White eh. By god lad, you'll be overtaking your dad next!

And where's the dog Uncle Dave? says Tom.

Gammy paw. Least it gives that one back at home something useful to do, looking after him.

Some of us look over at the Volvo again, but yes there's still only Pete there, resolutely facing forward as usual.

Dave smiles, punches Mum on the arm.

Alright?

Mum smiles, holds her arm a moment then nods at him and Marie, walks over to the car, peers in the back-door.

'Pete, no hug for your Aunty Grace then? Happy Birthday! Let's get going shall we?'

Becky in the back-room. Becky in the back-room. Becky in the back-

room. I'm staring at the ceiling again, they've taken all the electricals out and Dad has the key to the window. They're getting better at this, I'm going to have to raise my game. That ham salad sits congealing. Does Mum really expect me to? Look there's piccalilli on there and everything, for god's sake. I'm not to bother the guests am I. I'm not to bother. Not to. At all.

Not.

I am am am. I am here you lot. Whether you remember me or not. Misting up your window with my breath. Drawing.

Owwww goes the sound of my finger on the glass. Owwwww, making letters where there were none before, just condensation and mist, all the fug and rubbish of thousands of their stupid sounds hitting the window and turning to haze...Like E.T. here I lie and hide under blankets. Pose by sleeping Muggins and my bear.

I'm sure they'll be back soon.

Noooooo. I follow my finger's sound down the window. Noooooo, this is not happening. They wouldn't. They're not all that bad. That's what I've always said in my head.

Dad is very funny. A funny, funny man, everyone says, Dave Stephens. And Mum the best baker in this village by a country mile, according to everyone and including the fancy London man who gave our place three stars that now sit outside on a yellow and black plaque.

This is just one of those things. I broke the rules, no not the rules, it was the rule, and when you do that then you have to pay for a while. Like in Risk when you concentrate on one part of your strategy and let the other part slide, and then somebody suddenly invades.

No, not like that at all. This is not like anything really. A car rolls down next-door's drive - pull back the disgusting green and pink curtain. The lining is grubby, this is the room that is usually used for storage, not guests, not family.

Forgotten luggage.

Ha ha.

Despite everything, we're going the long way around. Past Janet's Foss and up to Gordale Scar before going around to the Cove. Five and a bit miles in all.

Can't miss out on a lovely day like this!

One of the adults waves an arm at the sky. It's a brilliant blue, and as we all walk through the green everyone already has their jumpers around their waists, all except the mums whose padded jackets always stays on no matter what and Pete who never seems to notice things like temperature, it's a boy thing; his dad was exactly the same at his age.

It's busy on the walk and all of the tourists are out, a procession of walking boots and t-shirts and people rustling in bags for crisps. We all file into the woods, a faint smell of garlic coming up from the carpet of ramsons, the clear water pulling little Tom over to its confines, as if magnetic.

Tom, back here!

Tom jumps off the mossy boulder and walks back up to the path slowly, kicking at a root, before running ahead as the adults talk about school again, voices rising up into the woodland:

How are you getting on this term then?

Same old, Marie, same old shenanigans with the time-tabling.

Murmuring voices run up and down as we push Pete on through the trees – it doesn't take much, just a hand on the back to keep him moving. His glacial expression remains the same as ever, but it seems like his eyes are playing him up a little as he's propelled through the green. Never mind. We stop at the waterfall, get our cameras out for the special birthday shot in front of the cascade. As ever there's almost a queue as people shuffle around each other in order to get their photos. Everyone, that is, except Pete who is standing staring at the waterfall from the middle of the boulder, getting in everyone's way.

Alright lad, says one man who's waiting to get a snap of his wife. Everything ok?

We look at each other, then at Pete who doesn't move, just stares at the water. We smile.

That's right son. It's your day today, isn't it.

Dave laughs and the women behind and in front turn and smile too, which is nice.

'Scuse me lad, could you?

The man is waiting still, he isn't smiling. A couple of us cough, others try to push Pete gently towards the wall on the left but he won't be pushed so the man gets a shot of his wife from far too close up then we all gather around Pete, smile as a woman in a pink zip-up fleece does the honours with the camera.

Cheeeese!

We crowd together to look: eight big grins and one dead gaze, and a man frowning off to the left.

Lovely! That'll be going on the wall next to the others.

We all pass around the Kendal Mint Cake before moving off towards the Scar.

But how can they...? I mean, am I really the only one...?

Anne's birthday, just this winter when we were last up near the waterfall. I was dead cold, we were all stamping our feet and blowing into our hands, all except Pete of course. I nudged Vic and said – look! – and she just looked away like she hadn't heard me, started in on Anne about some boy that she's apparently soft on. Luke, that's it.

Luke's nice, int he, she said. Then smiled and looked right through me as Anne hit her on the arm; like I hadn't said anything at all. And the whole time right next to her was Pete doing that weird thing. Like that's normal now, is it?

It was one thing when he started getting quieter. When was that? Must've been around two years ago, when he stopped wanting to beat me up whenever I beat him at Mario.

That's just the lad growing up, said Dad. Some get pensive Becky, I was quite retiring myself.

Then Pete's clothes started falling off him, we started going up to

BHS in Leeds for smaller jeans rather than bigger.

He looks like a famine victim, I said, Feed the World Mum.

She glared at me.

He's just going through a growth spurt, she said, crossing the folds of a brioche, some fancy recipe she'd picked up from her French book. It's making him thin out.

I tried to believe it. I mean, they want what's best for us don't they, so why would they call black, white or ignore what is plainly there in front of them?

I was sitting at the table reading my new Judy Blume when it happened. Dusk was falling outside and it was getting hard to see. Pete was just sitting at the table opposite me, staring out into the garden. I'd almost got used to that, you'd forget about him, it'd be like he wasn't there. But this time, even though Pete didn't move at some point I felt this pulsing from him, a revving up kind of energy as if something were happening inside him, something dead strange. I looked up and he was just staring but his normally light blue eyes were much darker. A purple colour, like something unearthly. Like they weren't his eyes. I screamed and pointed. Mum turned around from the sink. She put her hand over her heart and walked out of the room. I ran into the living room.

Did you see that Mum? Did you see what was happening to our Pete?

Mum was sitting perched on the end of the sofa, watching Stars in Your Eyes with Vicky, as if she'd been there all evening, as if Stars in Your Eyes were her favourite programme ever.

Mum?

She was laughing along to the crappy advert.

Mum!

Oh Becky, what is it now?

Did you see Pete?

What are you on about.

His eyes Mum. They've changed colour!

Vic laughed then Mum did too.

It's just the light child. Stop being such an attention seeker.

Then she turned and stared at me and Vic stared at me, then

Dad came in:

What are you harking on about now girl?

I turned and stomped upstairs, and when they all sat down to dinner, nobody came to get me.

I got quite hopeful when Dad was called up the school. Thought something might happen, finally, that would make things feel right again. I dunno, since all this Pete stuff started it's like I'm watching a movie and noticing all these things in it and all the others, they're watching the same movie but acting like it's some other movie. Anyway, there was a conversation with Mrs Sullivan and then suddenly Pete wasn't getting up with me in the mornings anymore.

Rubbish school anyway, said Uncle Tony. Terrible results at GCSEs last year, really shocking. He'll do much better at home.

As if that was the point. Morons. I should have known though, shouldn't I. Nobody ever said anything. Except me.

The mums are finally standing together as we all wait for Anne to climb up Gordale Scar. The shadow of the limestone cascade and rock face is a lovely respite after the heat of the walk; only Pete remains in the dusty sunlight back down by the creek. The rest of us stand at various points along the dark rocks at the bottom of the waterfall, watching Anne picking her way up the wet almost vertical boulders to the highest part of the first cascade.

Careful Anne!

From our various points under the shadow's yawn we shade our eyes with ours hands, look up. Anne shouts, waves but we can't hear her really, can just see her pink top, the sharp swing of her pony-tail as she twists to face the ascent again.

The mums are talking, finally. We're always listening for that happy sound, where-ever we're placed, wherever we are in the day.

I'd love to have that energy – she's a real live-wire your Anne isn't she.

Only sits to eat.

Vic used to be like that.

Yeah, that's right. Is she still playing badminton Vic?

Only just. On a Tuesday. But now Andy has to come too.

Oh right. Will I have to be buying myself a hat then?

Just keep an eye out, that's all I'm saying.

There is laughter and the mums look up, we all do: Anne has made it to the highest point of the Scar now. She waves and we all give little claps and whoops.

Well done Anne!

The rest of us begin to pick our way back across the rocks our bodies contorting as we look for sure footing. Tom is just one hop behind the men, shadowing their footsteps exactly, not missing one.

Down now Anne! Stop it!

One of us slips into a cold gap of water, a dark sliding place between the stones and stops, looks up a moment before carrying on. We are coming together; can hear the laughing, that gap between the two women entirely gone. Thank god. Their laughs climb higher, people start smiling as they pass our gathering group.

What's got into you two now?

The mums point up at the Scar - Anne is beating the air as if she's dancing at a rock concert.

Too many M&M's in the car that one.

They laugh properly now and it lifts us and the girls start joining in, a back and forth that feels like Christmas. Our eyes shine and we breathe the cool air deeply, pink rising to our cheeks now. Yes we're still the Wilkses and the Stephens, this togetherness between us still runs good and strong. This is what it's all about. These moments remain in stories that we can tell and re-tell at festive dos, climbing the stories like the steps up the side of that Scar into another good time. You can't pay for this, no amount of money could buy it, it doesn't matter who you are. This is our place. We're still smiling, Dave and Grace are still parrying, Marie and Vic joining in as we turn towards the sunny brook and the white dust of the footpath and someone motions to Anne to hurry up and get down for gods' sake and we all troop away -

Back to the birthday boy. He'll be needing those bumps soon.

We scan the many figures dotted around but Pete's dark form does not emerge. In the sunlight we stop and look back down the white path towards the ice-cream van, hands shading our eyes against the glare of the sun.

Nothing.

We bunch together and wait for Anne, Tom jumping up and down, the men chatting about the latest guests in Dave's B&B as Anne finally runs towards us, out of the shadows of the Scar.

Becky in the back-room, again. Becky in the back-room, AGAIN...

Yesterday's Ploughman's for dinner today. It sits across there congealing, the edges of the lettuce quivering in the waves from the radiator. We're never kept wanting for food for long round here, that I will say.

I wouldn't hold my tongue so I'm in here again today in case I ruin everything.

Scrape my finger dooooooooown the window, smudging out voices from the smokers on the drive. Dad's voice, all of their voices as they smoke their Christmas cigars. My head between two dirty curtains as I look up at the grey-white sky.

You should open a restaurant, called the man in the brown suit as he left the other day, Mum looking pink in the cheek by the back door as she waved him off.

She stands, waves off all the guests. Always waiting by the door like when the Wilkses all trooped up today for the all-important Christmas get-together. Wouldn't want to spoil that would I.

A procession of thumping feet through the hall. I can hear them talking in the kitchen now:

That's when we stopped for ice-creams at the Cove in the spring didn't we. That was a good one.

They'll be looking at that photo on the fridge – the one where Tom is raising up his ninety-nine with chocolate fudge, a blob of it on his nose. Next to that is the photo of Vic by a little lamb looking over the fields of the valley. Little white lamb with dirty knees, ears sticking up.

I still want to adopt one! I could bring it up.

Through the door I hear a rising tide of laughter as someone opens the fridge and there's a cheer - it must be the trifle - and then they move on through into the other room.

I think about that day in spring again, the day they all came home from the Cove.

They came back all together, the Wilkses crowding up the drive, not even looking towards my window. I counted everyone as they came up and into the house stamping their feet.

No Pete, I clocked it straight away.

The men went into the living room laughing, Jane and Vic away upstairs as usual. Mum and Aunt Marie went into the garden, in the gloom, Mum pointing out the forget-me-nots, where they've spread to. Her eyes were cold when she let me out of the room.

Supper then bed, she said, pointing to the kitchen.

Anne was at the table sitting like a zombie.

What happened? I whispered– sitting at the table. What happened Anne? Where's Pete?

Anne stared straight ahead.

Anne?

She walked into the next room and my heart stared beating really fast. As I passed the door on the way back to my room, I saw her pale, just sitting next to Dad on the sofa as he caught up with the football scores on Ceefax…

I'm boiling but can't open the window so I lick the condensation now, just to feel the cold. Seeing my breath hit the glass. Trying-to-get-out-

breath which has failed, lapping it up before it falls in tears down the window. Muggins wouldn't even do that. Muggins is out there though, isn't he. They wouldn't keep a dog cooped up for that long.

Cruel, says Dad.

He's a good man, funny man, they all say.

A few days ago I heard him on the phone to the opticians. Genial, as ever.

No, the lad's not living here at the moment. He's off staying with relatives and anyway his eyes are great, no bother.

So that's how the story goes now.

Merry Christmas Pete, I whisper. Merry Christmas lad, and I raise my tumbler to the violet sky feeling that revving feeling. Waiting.

Eventually it comes as somehow I knew it would. A tap tap tapping in the earliest light of dawn. I move over to the window as it begins to rattle.

In spring they're all up at Malham again, two spaces in the car this time.

We watch them by the ramsons, in the shadows of the fall. No matter how brilliant the sky, no matter how hard they laugh they can't help but glance over, even if they don't know why. Frowning a little as they shade their eyes against the sun.

COMPENSATING FOR EINSTEIN

Arnold Pettibone

After all that, it wasn't a government agency or any of the tech giants that cracked time travel. Not when they were all investing, almost exclusively, in anything that could provide clean drinking water and food. No, in the end it was a small team of theoretical physicists, labouring away in a crumbling office in the University of Southern Britain. An even bigger surprise was that there was even any research still going on, let alone non-commercial, but somehow there was and somehow they came up with this.

Now I don't pretend to understand how it works but, like most people, I've seen it on the news enough in the last few years to know the basics, at least. I watched that press conference a dozen times where the scientist, Damien Prince, drew a graph on a piece of paper, then rolled the paper into a funnel to demonstrate how two different points on the graph could be brought together. Someone in the press asked how Prince intended to roll the universe into a funnel. "By travelling faster than light," was the response that got the cameras clicking. The hapless journalist, as in the dark as most of his audience but nonetheless proud of his pre-prepared technical question, then asked how Prince and his team had compensated for the fact that the speed of light was a limiting factor, "as we have all known since Einstein." Prince smiled and struck a confident pose that made all that evening's newscasts. "I could explain it to you," he said, "but you wouldn't understand. Suffice to say we can compensate for Einstein."

What was left of the serious press – the few that still had dedicated science correspondents - explored this claim in more detail, and gushed about Minkowski space, pseudo-Riemannian manifolds and Möbius geometry. It all seemed very plausible. Someone in the less serious press coined the phrase "Einstein compensator" and that was still being used in the headlines when Prince and his team claimed the last Nobel prize for physics.

As it turned out, there were some limiting factors; real world time travel is much different to the fictional version in films and books. For a start, because there are some constants involved – the speed of light, for one, and the diameter of a hydrogen nucleus, for another – it seems you can only travel a fixed amount of time. From memory, I think the exact figure is 48.17 years; what I know for sure is that the media called this the 50 year limit. Even more limiting, The Prince method can only be used to travel forward in time, not backwards, Einstein compensator or not. Apparently it is easy to roll spacetime into a positive funnel but not a negative one. I have no idea what a negative funnel might be, and I guess that's why I'm not a physicist.

Anyway, the one-way nature of the Prince method was a big relief for everyone, not least for the hastily convened United Nations Committee for Temporal Affairs; no-one was going to be travelling back in time and altering anything. Like I said, real time travel is very different to the fictional version. But more than that, the forwards-only limit means that time travel really is a one-way ticket. Yes, you can hop 48.17 years into the future … but you can't come back again.

Which means, of course, that although it is proven in theory and demonstrated in practice, it is not proven in practice. Things have been sent forward in time using the Prince method, sure. In a now famous but very obvious publicity stunt, the first item publicly sent forward in time was a framed photograph of Einstein – you know the picture where he's sticking his tongue out? And it certainly went somewhere. There was a lot of build-up, the world was watching, there was a countdown, Prince flipped a switch, and then … the picture just disappeared. No light show, no flames, no sound effects. The picture just ceased to be here, now.

Of course, that doesn't mean it worked. That first public demo was nearly ten years ago, so we all have to wait another forty years for definitive proof that it was successful.

After that, public interest waned – some started to question whether they should believe something worked, just because someone smarter than them said it had. Others decried the lack of physical proof – you could have all the theoretical proof in the world, and as many equations as you liked, but without physical proof… Conspiracy theorists were quick to point out that all the Prince method actually seemed to do was obliterate anything that was fed into it. There were, of course, other public demonstrations, each more outlandish than the last, in the hope of generating continued interest and, presumably, funding. Bigger and more complex items were sent forward. Then some live tests were conducted, first with a Petri dish full of mould, then some earth worms, I think. Finally, a dog was loaded into the machine, a button was pushed and, without fanfare or fuss, he was gone. Banjo, the dog's name was.

There was a bit of an outcry from various activists over that. The Committee for Temporal Affairs called an extraordinary meeting. From then on, time travel slipped gradually off the radar, dismissed as an unproven curio, nothing more really than an expensive way of disappearing and, who knows, maybe dying.

And that's how it might have remained, a footnote in science history, if not for Prince's suicide last year.

Except that suicide isn't really the right word for it, given what was discovered later. Sure, he left a note, in which he wrote of his despair at the state of the world, and of wanting to go "to a better place". But no body was ever found. More than that, when police forced their way into his lab, they found the latest version of his time travel apparatus powered up. Prince's research associates were able to confirm from telemetry and audit logs that the machine had last been used on the same day that their boss had left his note. Not only that but it had been configured for a mass of 75.6kg. Hence the assumption that Prince had sent himself through his machine – that his better place was simply the future.

What no-one predicted, when this was first reported, was that others would want to follow suit. Would literally be queuing up for the opportunity to send themselves God knew where on the basis of unproven physics. But that's exactly what happened. At first it was dressed up as individuals bestowing grant funding on the university, in exchange for a place on a trial. But soon all pretence was abandoned, not least because by turning it into a commercial operation rather than a research project the university no longer had to wrestle with ethics committees.

And so, for the last six months, people have been lining up to part with their life savings for a shot at something that *might* be better: a one-way ticket to the future. Or maybe, just maybe, a one-way ticket to oblivion.

Like most people, I've watched this happen with a sense

of slightly incredulous, morbid fascination. I mean, I know things are pretty bad right now, but even so? Yes, I'm tired of crowds and queuing, of rationing, of forced relocations and emergency billeting. I can't remember when I last ate normal food, rather than the eezy-squeezy they pump out at the food station. But I'm tired of the black market too. I'm tired of boiling water and waiting for it to cool. I'm tired of checking the weather forecast and flood warnings four times a day. I'm tired of the heat. And I'm tired of never having enough energy credits to keep even the basics turned on.

So we talked about it, Sally and I. Turns out she was even more tired than I was. "Everything's gone to pot," she said, "everything. So why not go somewhere, some*when* else, where some of these problems will have been solved." Now I didn't want to rain on her parade, especially since it was the first time I had seen her look enthusiastic or excited about anything for a very long time. So I didn't say the obvious, which was that maybe we wouldn't go anywhere, or that even if it actually worked and we got shuttled forward 50 years, maybe things would be even worse. I just made the right noises, and thought it was a flight of fancy. But when she came back a week later with news that she'd found a company who'd buy our house, I knew she was serious. It's a ridiculous price – 30 grand is nothing, but even the most optimistic predictions show our little plot being underwater in twelve years. The pessimistic forecast is eight years, so to find any sort of buyer is miraculous, really. In all likelihood, it'll be one of those roof-pushers who'll strip the house bare, fill it with pods and cram as many refugees in as they can, charge them all extortionate rent and then leave them to fend for themselves when the tide inevitably crashes in and washes the whole place away.

Whatever, the bottom line is that we've agreed to sell the house and cash everything else in too. Between us, we can just about get enough together to go, and Sal has already applied for our places and paid a deposit – we are 1,137 and 1,138 in the queue, but I still can't believe we're really going. There's a part of me that is genuinely excited – it's the same part that's tired of this life at the arse end of the 21st Century on this grey and blue planet, if you can call it living. I know, me and 15 billion others, right? And there's a part of me that's scared too – I've read up on the Prince method as much as possible, and think I understand it as well as a non-physicist can, but it's still just a theory, a concept waiting to be proven by the reappearance of Einstein's tongue-out photograph in 40 years. But what if it doesn't work, and we've just signed ourselves up to be vaporised?

Most of all though, I'm worried where we'll end up if it works. Sally's an optimist, no easy feat these days, but she thinks that necessity is the mother of invention and that mankind will work everything out in time: turn back the tides, irrigate and refertilise the soil, freeze the ice-caps, grow enough real food for everyone, stabilise the water supply, cool the planet … all of that. "People are smart," she said to me, last night. "With enough time and enough resources, there's nothing that can't be fixed. We're just going to hop ahead and cut out the fixing!" She smiled after that, the sort of smile that's been missing since … well, since we were teenagers. And I didn't have the heart to say what was really on my mind. Which was that even if the Prince method works, and we successfully reappear in 48.17 years, who's to say anything will be any better? And couldn't things conceivably be a lot worse? What if the Earth is like a piece of elastic – stretch it so far and it will still spring back to its default state, but stretch it *too* far and it's deformed forever. What if the Earth's elastic has snapped?

I'm going to leave this behind when we go. It feels a bit old-fashioned and also extravagant to write it on paper but I've been saving this notepad for a special occasion; I think this, my version of Prince's note, qualifies. I don't know what our future holds but one thing I do know is this: you think it's crowded here now, Sally, just wait until you see it in 50 years' time.

See you on the other side.

ABOUT THE AUTHORS

Mark Kilner

Mark is an author, astronomer and wildlife photographer. His short story *The Evaluation* was the winner of the 2018 British Fantasy Society Short Story Competition. His three short story collections, *Let's Kill Love*, *Numbskulls*, and *Process of Elimination*, are available in paperback & eBook from www.amazon.co.uk/Mark-Kilner/e/B00FBFRAXY

Ian Nettleton

Ian Nettleton is from the north of England but he has lived in Norwich for two decades. His long short story, *Falling Star*, was published in a science fiction anthology, *Angles*, in 2008 and his novel, *The Last Migration*, was runner-up in the inaugural Bath Novel Award 2014 and runner-up in the inaugural Bridport Prize Peggy Chapman-Andrews Award 2014. He is represented by Sue Armstrong of the Conville and Walsh literary agency. He has a PhD in Creative and Critical Writing from the University of East Anglia and teaches creative writing at the Open University (prose, scriptwriting, life writing and poetry at undergraduate and MA level), the National Centre for Writing and the University of East Anglia. He is currently editing a literary thriller set in Queensland, Australia, called *Out of Nowhere*, an excerpt of which appears in this anthology. His website can be found at iannettleton.weebly.com and he is also on Twitter @IanNettletonUK

Andrea Holland

Andrea Holland is a Lecturer in Creative Writing at the University of East Anglia. Her collection of poems, *Broadcasting* (Gatehouse Press, 2013) was a winner of the Norfolk Commission for Poetry. Her first collection *Borrowed*, was published by Smith/Doorstop in 2007. She has poems in *MsLexia, The Rialto, The North* and other literary journals as well as online, and has contributed chapters to books and articles on creative writing. She has also collaborated with visual artists on a number of commissioned projects. Andrea resides in Norwich with her family, after studying and teaching in the USA for a number of years. www.andreacholland.co.uk

Katy Carr

Katy Carr is currently working on a novel called *Back to the River*, set in the Brecklands. Her first novel, *Under*, is currently on submission. She is studying on the Lancaster MA in Creative Writing and works in literature and marketing.

Sandy Greenard

Sandy Greenard completed her Diploma in Creative Writing at the University of East Anglia in 2009. In her spare time Sandy continues to write short stories and give lectures on Dutch Art. Having moved to Ufford, near Woodbridge, Sandy is now responsible for the planning and implementation of the 2018 Ufford Arts Festival.

Rol Hirst

For almost 40 years, Rol dreamed of being a published writer. Then one day he abandoned that fantasy and embraced fatherhood as a far less soul-destroying way of achieving immortality. Maybe he'll write again when he retires, if the grave doesn't claim him first. For now, he manages the withdrawal symptoms by writing a daily music blog with nine reluctant readers.

Rol's debut novel *I Wish, Wish, Wish You Were Dead, Dead, Dead* is available in paperback and eBook from www.amazon.co.uk/dp/B00EOAG1WI/

Simon Poore

Simon is a tall writer and musician from Norfolk, with an enviable collection of impressive hats. You can discover more at simontall.com

Sarah Dobbs

Sarah is a lecturer in Creative Writing at the University of Sunderland, where she also runs the Short Story Award in

Association with Waterstones. Her first novel was *Killing Daniel* (Unthank Books) and she also editor of a textbook *How to Pass your Degree in English Language, Literature and Creative Writing* (Anthem Press). She's working on a new novel and a collection. Follow her @sarahjanedobbs

Martin Pond

Martin is a Man of Kent, now living and working in Norfolk. In addition to editing this collection, his stories have appeared in *Unthology No 1* (Unthank Books), *Streetcake* magazine and *Alliterati* magazine. In 2012, Martin was a winner of Comma Press's Short Story Day "story in ten words or less" competition. *Drawn To The Deep End*, Martin's first novel, was published in September 2017, and can be found at amzn.to/martinpond - you can also follow Martin on Twitter @martinwrites

Ada Carter

Ada Carter loves the outdoors and all things writerly. She lives and works in Norfolk and London. Do send any hellos through the editor.

Arnold Pettibone

Arnold Pettibone spends a lot of time thinking about the future. *Compensating for Einstein* is his first (and possibly last) published story.

ABOUT POPULATION MATTERS

Population Matters is a membership charity that addresses population size and environmental sustainability. It believes population growth contributes to environmental degradation, resource depletion, poverty and inequality. It promotes smaller families and sustainable consumption across the world, to achieve a healthy planet and a decent standard of living for all.

The charity (originally called the Optimum Population Trust) was founded in 1991 in the United Kingdom and now has thousands of members across dozens of countries. Population Matters' vision is of a sustainable future with decent living standards, a healthy environment and a stable population size. It campaigns, informs, undertakes research and does all it can to encourage an open, fair-minded and constructive debate about population.

Population Matters supports human rights, gender equality and global justice. It opposes any coercive measures to limit population growth or people's freedom to choose to have a family. The charity believes that population is not just an issue in those places where population growth is highest: people in all countries have a responsibility to bring their populations to sustainable levels as soon as they can by ethical means. That means that where consumption and environmental impact is high, as it is in the developed world, each of us must consider the impact of our family size.

www.populationmatters.org

Printed in Great Britain
by Amazon